Just Add Romance

AN
Everly Falls
NOVEL

Just Add Romance

HEATHER B. MOORE

Mirror Press

Just Add Romance was previously published under the title *Loving Her Fling*. No part of this book may be reproduced in any form whatsoever without prior written permission of the publisher, except in the case of brief passages embodied in critical reviews and articles. This is a work of fiction. The characters, names, incidents, places, and dialogue are products of the author's imagination and are not to be construed as real.

Interior design by Cora Johnson
Edited by JL Editing Services and Lorie Humpherys
Cover design by Rachael Anderson
Cover image credit: Deposit Photos #24894003 by Anskuw
Published by Mirror Press, LLC

ISBN: 978-1-952611-28-5

Just Add Romance

No commitment? He can do that. A fling? She can do that.
There's no harm in adding a little romance.

Everly Kane's life might be on a Plan B track, but she's
perfectly content with her job, her nights out at the movies,
and putting her past behind her. She certainly doesn't need to
be reminded over and over that her sister is, well, engaged to
Everly's ex. Spending time with the visiting architect in town
is the distraction that she needs.

Austin Hayes is the architect hired to redesign Everly's
beloved theater. As a widower with a young daughter, the last
thing he wants is to juggle another relationship.

Thankfully, Austin is only in Everly Falls for a few weeks.
What could be better than having a fling with a guy who has
no power to break her heart?

One

IT WASN'T THAT EVERLY KANE didn't want a man in her life, it was more like she hadn't found one without a major flaw. And by major, she meant someone who was still in love with his ex-wife, or still lived with his parents, or insisted on being called by his gaming name, Pete-87.

Unfortunately, Everly had dated each of those type of men at least once. The guy in love with his ex? Twice. Different guys, same major flaw.

And . . . this made it easier for Everly not to feel guilty when inventing a budding relationship on the phone with her mother. Especially when her younger sister's wedding was in three weeks.

"Honey," her mother murmured into the phone. "Are you sure you're okay? You sound upset."

"I'm fine, Mom," Everly said. "Really. I'm exhausted from work and class." Truthfully, she hadn't wanted to answer her mom's phone call because she'd just pulled up to the Everly Falls movie theater. It was a Wednesday night, and very few people would be at the movies, exactly how Everly liked it.

Oh, and that's right, Everly was named after her own town. It was a joke that got very old, very fast, in grade school. She pushed the thought away.

The movie started in ten minutes, and unlike the rest of the general population in America, she loved the previews. She'd analyze each one, then mark in her Notes app whether the upcoming movies were a must-see, see-only-if-nothing-else-good-is-playing, or a hard-pass.

Everly also needed about eight minutes to buy a ticket, get popcorn and soda, then be in her seat before the lights dimmed. It was part of the transition from real world to movie world. It gave her goosebumps every time.

"All right, honey," her mom continued, in a sympathetic tone that had gotten on Everly's nerves lately. "We'll see you tomorrow at the bridal shower, all right? And you can tell us all about this mystery man you're dating. Tom, is it? What's his last name?"

"Uh, Middleston." Everly winced. Had she channeled the actor she was about to watch in one of the Avengers movies? Their town theater had two auditoriums—one showed new releases, the other showed oldies, but goodies.

"Wonderful, dear," her mother said. "We'll look forward to hearing all about Tom Middleston tomorrow."

Everly's voice was very, very small when she said, "Okay, bye Mom." She hung up, the small pit in her stomach feeling like it had grown to a full-sized apple now.

Was it so horrible to pretend that she was dating someone? She'd had pretend boyfriends before—guys she'd talked about when she was in middle school and high school—when the popular girls were throwing around words like *dating, kissing, holding hands*... Once Everly had declared she had a boyfriend, who lived in her cousin's town, so she only got to see him on family visits, and suddenly, Everly wasn't the frumpy girl in school with the wild, curly hair. She was the interesting girl.

Everly sighed and climbed out of her car. The wind was warm for June, and it stirred her messy bun, making it even messier.

A pretend boyfriend was probably fine when she was a teenager. But now? At twenty-seven? Perhaps not so fine.

But desperate times called for desperate measures, right?

As in when your gorgeous little sister, Brandy, was getting married in a few weeks to the equally gorgeous Brock Hayes. Who was pretty much amazing in every way, expect for one tiny detail. One tiny, but significant detail.

He was Everly's ex-boyfriend.

She pushed down the bitterness that she'd kept firmly buried and tucked her jacket under her arm as she crossed the nearly empty parking lot. It might be a warm June night, but she always brought a jacket for the theater. She adjusted her messy bun, which she'd once had decent before work that day. She thought her job at the craft store was fun, but her mother didn't think so and considered it an aimless career.

But Everly loved the organized aisles of craft items and the potential in each item to create something unique. It combated the topsy-turvy world of expectations outside the craft shop. Even in her sleepy town, it seemed that everyone was living a full, accomplished life. Her girlfriends from high school were either in great careers or getting married. Or married with a kid. Or . . .

Everly pulled open the theater door as her cell phone buzzed with a text.

OMG, Mom told me you're dating someone! I want to hear all about it!

The text, alas, was from Brandy. There was no way Everly could carry on this fib any longer. Her mom might believe her,

3

but Brandy would see through it in an instant. Everly sighed, and without opening the text—so her sister wouldn't know she'd read it—she turned off her phone. Another rule she had about going to the movies. No phones. No distractions.

She bought her ticket at the snack counter.

"Hi, Everly," Janlyn said. She was a teenager who worked at the snack counter, her dark, soulful eyes rarely smiled.

Which is why Everly made sure to greet her cheerfully. "Great to see you, Jan. How's everything going?"

"Oh, you know, the same."

It was the same—the same response she always gave.

"Oh, okay," Everly said. "Ticket for one, please. I'm seeing the Avengers."

"The usual snacks?"

Which was a medium popcorn and medium Dr. Pepper. Yep. Everly had a standing order at the movie theater. She nodded sheepishly and tapped on the counter while she waited.

Jan returned a moment later with both snacks.

Everly picked everything up and headed toward the theater room. Her hands were full, so she used her shoulder to push through the door. She'd been right. Only a handful of other people were inside. She picked her favorite spot— middle aisle, middle seat. The only way to get the full effect of course.

She briefly toyed with the thought of turning on her phone and answering her sister, but then a string of texts would follow. The lights would be dimming any minute, and Everly didn't want the distraction. Besides, she still hadn't made up the story of how she'd met Tom—ahem, Middleston—or what he looked like, etc.

Just as the lights lowered, a tall man walked into the theater. Alone. A quick glance told Everly that he was one of those confident, good-looking types. He had brownish hair that was long enough to touch his collar, deep-set eyes, broad shoulders, and he was built yet lean. He probably had a girlfriend or wife joining him any minute. Which meant that Everly should not be checking him out. But she'd never seen him before, and she knew everyone in town.

Was he passing through town? Here on a work trip? Visiting his in-laws?

His clothing was generic for the most part—jeans that fit him quite nicely, and a gray or blue t-shirt beneath a darker colored jacket.

The theater went dark then, illuminated only by the screen showing a commercial reminding everyone to silence their phones and be respectful of their neighbors.

The tall man hadn't found a seat yet, but remained near the entrance, as if he were scanning the chairs.

Maybe he was picky like her? Everly's gaze shifted back to the screen as a movie trailer started, it was some thriller with a bunch of teenagers in it. She dug her small notebook out of her bag and jotted down the title of the movie, ranking it a three—middle of the road.

The man was still standing by the entrance, scanning seats.

Sit down already, Everly wanted to say. The second trailer started, one of those high-action car chase movies. She wrote down the title, then ranked it a one—a must-see.

The man started forward, and soon he climbed the steps, getting closer to her middle row. She fully expected him to continue on past her row, but he didn't. He turned right into her row.

Everly didn't move. Couldn't. There were literally dozens of empty rows.

Yet, the man with the broad shoulders and well-fitted

jeans continued down *her* row, getting closer and closer to her. Until he stopped.

Everly's breathing stopped with him. No, she didn't turn her head, but she could very well see him in her peripheral vision. She knew exactly how many seats away he sat from her when he sat down.

Two.

Two

AUSTIN HAYES HAD WANTED TO turn down this job. Renovating an old theater in a small town closer to his home would have been fine. But not in Everly Falls. The theater itself was charming, although severely outdated. From the moment he walked into the building he could smell the decades-old popcorn grease, but beyond that, he was already calculating the amount of work that would need to be done.

Tomorrow, he'd get a copy of the blueprints from Town Hall, and that's when the real calculations would begin.

Tonight, he was coming to the theater as a regular moviegoer. To check things out from a distance and to gauge his first impressions.

His dad had apparently visited relatives in Everly Falls as a kid, and he was the type to keep in touch with friends over the years. So, the city council had contacted his dad about the job. According to him, there was something sentimental about the place. The problem was, his dad's hip surgery had put him out of commission for a couple of months, and possibly for much longer. So here Austin was instead of his dad. A

7

hundred miles away from home on a two-to-three-month job. Which meant that there would be few chances to see his seven-year-old daughter, Jessica. Thankfully, his mom had stepped in to help with Jessica.

Being away from Jessica so much hadn't been the path he wanted. Of course, that had been the pattern of his life the past few years. When his wife had died from cancer a couple of years ago, that had definitely not been the path he'd chosen. Becoming a single dad with a young daughter had not been his plan. Neither had the long and lonely months that had followed when his mother's friends, and his mother herself, had tried to set him up with one woman or another.

Everyone had given him space for about six months, then the interference set in.

"Jessica needs a mother," Austin's mom had said with more and more frequency. "We all miss Rachel, but it's okay to move on. She would have wanted that for you."

But Austin rarely had free time, and when he did, Jessica was his priority. Still, he had been on a handful of token dates, and honestly, none of them had struck him as mother material for Jess. He'd even kissed one of the women, and she'd then wanted to move past all of the relationship steps and move in together.

No thanks.

Once Austin was settled into his seat at the theater, he tried to forget everything for a few hours. A woman sat a couple of seats over in the seat he would normally have preferred. Middle of the middle was always the best seat in a theater. Rachel used to tease him about it.

Memories like that made him miss her. During the early days of their marriage, that was. Times like this, when it was just him, and he wasn't focused on work, the good memories flooded back. Despite the opening action scenes of the most recent Avengers movie, Austin was barely paying attention. Although the not-so-good memories were more recent, when he thought of Rachel, he tried to think only of their early marriage together.

They had always been in sync. Loved the same foods, the same recreation, the same type of decorating for their house . . . Eventually, though, their lives had become routine, predictable, even *boring*. Just as Rachel had accused him of being.

She wanted a baby as much as he did, and when Jessica was born, they both doted on her. The first couple of years, anyway. Then Rachel went back to work at a salon, and things slowly shifted in their relationship. She had started spending more and more time after work with her coworkers. They'd meet for dinners and girls-only weekend events.

Austin didn't mind at first, until the day Rachel announced that she was going to start staying over a few nights a week at Taylor's so that she didn't have to deal with the hairy commute. Austin was dead set against it because Jessica needed her mom and her dad.

But Rachel wouldn't budge. Then four months later, she was diagnosed with cancer.

One week after the funeral, a man named Taylor called Austin, asking him to come and fetch Rachel's things. It turned out that the woman Taylor, was really a *man* named Taylor.

"Excuse me, sir?" someone said above him.

It took Austin a moment to realize he had fallen asleep in the movie theater, and the movie was now over. He blinked open his eyes to see a woman standing above him. He guessed her to be the same woman from his row.

Had he been dreaming about Rachel? He hadn't even realized he'd fallen asleep. Yeah, he was tired, but still, *Avengers* should have kept him conscious.

9

"Sir? Do you speak English?"

"Uh, yeah." His voice was raspy from his impromptu nap.

The woman gazed at him, her head tilted and hazel eyes curious. Her dark blonde hair was a riot of curls and braids with metal things on them, pulled up into a messy bun. And her clothing . . . he wasn't sure he'd ever seen so many different colors on a single person before. Her top was dark pink, and her jacket was some sort of yellow. Her red jeans followed her curves like they'd been painted on.

"The theater has cleared out," she said, her tone low and mellow.

Austin nodded, although his head still felt heavy from sleep. "Thanks, I guess I fell asleep." The screen was completely dark as if the credits had finished rolling too.

Instead of moving on, like most people might—most strangers that was—the woman said, "Long day?"

"You could say that." Austin rose to his feet and stifled a yawn.

The woman still hadn't left.

She was several inches shorter than him, yet he guessed that her personality was far from small. She carried a shoulder bag that looked more like a folded quilt, and in one hand she held an empty popcorn container with a drink container inside of that.

"Well, you shouldn't be driving then," she said. "There's a bed and breakfast down the block if you need a place to stay."

Everly Falls must be one of those places where everyone knew everyone. "I have a place, thanks." He took a step forward, expecting the woman to step out of the way, but she didn't move.

He supposed he could go down the opposite way.

"Oh, sorry," the woman said. "I didn't mean to hold you

hostage or anything." She took a step back, then turned and moved along the row.

Austin followed at a bit of a distance. In her wake, he could smell whatever perfume she was wearing. Or was it her shampoo, or lotion? Whatever it was, it was sweet, and quite nice.

He kept his gaze up, not on her swaying hips or those heeled sandals of hers.

She walked quickly, and he was surprised at her speed. He wondered how long she had waited to wake him up because when he reached the lobby, the entire place was empty. Not a single employee was in sight.

The woman had already reached the exit doors, and she pushed through them without looking back. Austin decided there must be someone coming to lock up later, so he left the building too.

"Oh!" a woman exclaimed.

The same woman . . . Austin looked over and saw that she had fallen on the curb leading to the parking lot.

"Are you okay?" he asked as he strode over, although she was already sitting up and didn't appear injured.

"Oh no," she muttered and began to scramble on the ground. Her giant purse had spilled.

"I can help," Austin said, crouching to gather what looked like small squares of paper.

"Careful," she said. "Don't let them get bent."

"What are these?" Austin asked, holding one up so he could read the printed words in the outside lights of the movie theater. It was a movie ticket stub.

"My movie stubs," she said, then rose to her feet and chased after a couple that were blowing in the breeze. "My box must have popped open when I dropped my bag."

She returned, out of breath, her hair even more wild, her breathing hard.

Austin handed her what he'd gathered.

"Thanks," she said, tucking them into what looked like a plastic pencil box. "I'd hate to lose my collection."

Austin should probably head to his truck, but he'd never heard of a grown woman collecting movie stubs. "How long have you been collecting?"

Her gaze lifted to his, and he was pretty sure he'd never seen eyelashes that long. At least not natural ones. Rachel had been all about the fake eyelashes until she developed some sort of allergy to the glue.

"Since my first movie."

Austin's brows popped up. "You have all the stubs in there from every movie you've ever attended?"

"No," the woman said. "These are about two years' worth. I wouldn't carry around that many movie tickets."

Austin didn't know if he should laugh or continue staring at her. "You're kind of a movie buff, huh?"

She set her box inside her bag, then shouldered it and met his gaze. "I'm a secret movie buff," she said. "That's why I'm here on Wednesday nights. Place is mostly empty."

"Do you always sit in the middle seat, in the middle of the theater?" he asked.

She smiled.

Her smile was beautiful.

Which was something he probably shouldn't be noticing. Along with how he was rather enjoying her flowery scent. And . . . he took a step back because he suddenly realized how close he was to this stranger.

"I do." She tilted her head. "And you? I almost thought you were going to ask me to move."

He laughed. "I wouldn't, because that would be rude."

She was still smiling. "It is the best seat in the theater."

"Agreed."

She folded her arms, and the series of bracelets along her arms jangled. "Are you new in town? Passing through?"

"Neither," he said. "I'm here to renovate the theater."

Three

EVERLY GASPED. ALOUD. "W-WHAT?"

The guy with the brown hair, broad shoulders, and oh-so-chocolatey eyes, had turned out to be a gentleman. Until now.

"I'm the architect with Hayes Architecture," he said. "The town of Everly Falls hired us to get the thing in shape."

Her mouth opened, then closed, then opened again. How was this possible? The theater couldn't be changed, or touched in any way. She had been to the modern theaters where everything was shiny and gray. If she was going to be reduced to that, she might as well stay home and watch Netflix.

"You can't," she said finally.

The man's brows pulled together, which made him no less handsome. *Dang it.*

"I ... *can't?*" he said. "Do you work for the town council or something?"

"No," she said. "I work at the craft store, but I'm a *very* invested citizen in this theater. And I knew nothing of this ... renovation." Heat was quickly crawling up her neck. "I never heard of a town vote on it."

14

His mouth quirked, and the heat along her skin intensified.

"I don't know if it went to a vote or not," he said smoothly, calmly, like she was a little child, "but I can assure you that the renovation is planned and budgeted for."

Was he laughing at her?

She pulled her bag closer to her body as if it would give her some stability. "So, what are the plans then?"

"That's what I'll be spending the next couple of days doing," he said. "I have to head to the Town Hall in the morning. Although, I do have a few ideas."

Everly's mind raced. "Like what?"

He gave her a strange look, but she didn't blink, didn't break her gaze. "Uh, who are you, again?"

"I said I work at the craft store," she said.

"What's your name?"

She released a tiny exhale. He'd learn her name soon enough since she planned to file a complaint about this renovation. "Everly."

"Everly? As in . . .?"

"Yes."

He paused, and she waited for him to say it. Instead, he said, "Is . . . Everly short for something? Beverly?"

"No. Just Everly. And what's your name, sir?"

His brows lifted slightly, but he said, "Austin Hayes."

"*Hayes?*" Her voice might have risen an octave, or more. What were the chances that Austin Hayes was related to the Everly Falls Hayes, aka the man her sister was going to marry in a few weeks. "Do you know Brock Hayes?"

To his credit, he looked confused. "Does he live around here?"

"Yes."

"My dad has some relatives here," Austin said. "I've never met them, though. Second cousins, or something."

So that was sort of a relief. Why she cared exactly, she didn't know.

"Is Brock a movie buff too?"

She should cut to the chase. "He's my sister's fiancé." No matter how many times she said it, or thought it, she felt a pang right in the center of her chest. "Well, I guess I'll see you tomorrow then."

Austin's brown eyes narrowed. "You will?"

"Yes, I'll be at the Town Hall, too," she said, taking a step away. Then another.

His gaze had turned curious, and Everly ignored how pleased that made her feel. A man curious about what she might say. Imagine that.

"I'll be there filing a complaint." She turned then and headed across the parking lot.

Austin Hayes didn't say anything, but she felt his gaze on her all the way to her car.

And seeing that there was only one other vehicle in the parking lot—a white truck—she now knew what he was driving.

She was quite proud of herself for staying within the speed limit while driving home. Well, home was a relative word. She lived in a makeshift apartment above the craft store. Makeshift because there weren't really four walls. There were three, and two-thirds to be exact. The stairs that led from the store to the second level comprised that partial wall.

There had been a time or two that a customer had opened the staircase door and wandered right into her living quarters. Now, there was a large sign on that door that read, *Do Not Enter.* Everly opened the do-not-enter door and trudged up the steps, flipping on the light as she went.

Meow.

Everly looked up to see her beloved Snatches waiting

stubbornly at the top of the stairs for her. No, the cat wouldn't come down even one step.

"Hello, sweetie," Everly said, arriving on the landing and combing through Snatches' sleek fur.

The cat had been a work in progress. Nine months ago, it had shown up on her windowsill. The windowsill of Everly's second-floor living space. At first, she thought she'd finally lost all her marbles and was seeing cats appearing out of nowhere. But upon closer inspection, after sliding open the window and popping out the screen, she saw that one of the trees outside the craft shop was a perfect climbing tree that led right to her window.

Which was how the cat got there.

The little orange tabby had rumbled with loud purrs, and no one could have blamed Everly for taking the tiny thing into her place and promptly feeding her a bowl of milk.

Snatches had been devoted ever since. Well, in the snatches of time Everly saw her. Everly was busy most of the time, and the cat disappeared often, but always returned with a lot of purring and a huge appetite.

"Let's get you fed, sweetie," Everly crooned.

The cat could apparently understand human English because she trotted to the half-sized fridge.

Everly smiled and pulled out a carton of milk, added it to a clean bowl, then set it down on the floor. Next, she scooped some premium cat food into another fresh bowl. Nine months ago, Everly might have scoffed at pet owners spoiling their fur babies, but no longer.

Snatches had brought a new brightness to her life.

In fact, now that she thought about it, Snatches had shown up the day after Everly's breakup with Brock.

And Snatches had been there for Everly during the days following her sister's tearful confession that she and Brock had been secretly dating. Granted, they hadn't started dating until a few months after the break-up, but there wasn't much consolation in that.

It had been a while since Everly had a sleepless night wondering if, during all the times Brock had been with her family, he had been secretly checking out her sister. Even their names went together better—Brandy and Brock. Brock and Brandy.

"Do you have a sister, Snatches?" Everly asked, bending to scratch the adorable fluffy head.

Snatches arched with a rumbling purr, then settled back to her food.

Brandy and Everly had been inseparable during their childhood, and it was only when Everly had gone to college that they'd each grown into their own, separate personalities. Two semesters majoring in art had been about all Everly could stand of the rigorous schedule, and she'd returned to Everly Falls. Oh, and a breakup with Jim. Jim the Jerk, as she now referred to him in her mind.

Everly Falls was a different town as an adult. Brandy had already started her freshman year at a different college, and so the sisters remained separated for the most part. Everly had worked at the grocery store, then the bakery, followed by a failed stint at the diner. Dating Brock had made her feel like her life was moving forward.

Brock, who was dark haired, dark eyed, quick to laugh, and made everything fun . . . And then Brandy came home for Christmas, no longer the kid sister, but all grown up and beautiful.

Had it started then?

Looking back, Everly could only wonder. Nothing had been a red flag, but maybe it was because she wasn't paying attention to whether her boyfriend was crushing on her younger sister. Brandy, who even at twenty-four had her life together, with her accounting degree, her start-up nonprofit business well on its way, and her slim figure and lustrous straight hair. Her clear blue eyes and long lashes. Who could eat whatever she wanted, but had the discipline to run miles every day.

Meow.

"Yeah, me too," Everly said absentmindedly to the cat.

She settled onto her loveseat and fished out her cell phone, then turned it on. The texts from her sister were glaring, and for a moment, Everly felt bad about her little white lie to her mom. Okay, so maybe it wasn't little. But it would get her mom and her sister and all their nosy cousins off her back about dating someone.

Obviously, the second she'd hung up with her mom earlier that night, her mom had told her sister. Thus, the myriad texts.

Truthfully, Everly was tired of the pitying looks, the whispered words, and the knowing glances. Because Everly had not only been dumped, but her boyfriend had proposed to her sister.

Snatches jumped up on Everly's lap and kneaded her claws into Everly's thighs. "Ouch, you brat."

Snatches ignored her and continued kneading, completely content.

Everly scratched the top of the cat's head, then scanned through her sister's multiple texts.

Let's get together tonight, you can tell us all about him. Or bring him too!

Everly knew that *us* meant Brock. Brandy was always with Brock.

Brandy's next text read: *Where are you? At the dumpy theater again? At least text us a picture of Tom!*

What was up with *us* again? Was Brandy no longer her own person? Did every conversation have to include Brock and Brandy together?

The cat curled up in her lap, so it looked like Everly would be stuck on her loveseat for a bit. She texted her sister back: *I'm calling you now.*

Brandy answered on the first ring, her voice breathless with excitement. "I'm soo happy for you!"

"Hang on, Sis," Everly said. "I might have exaggerated the truth to Mom."

"What do you mean?" Brandy asked, her tone a little less peppy now.

"Well, uh, here's the thing," Everly began, then told her sister all about the made-up boyfriend with the pathetic name.

Brandy laughed. Hard. And she didn't seem to be stopping any time soon. When she finally did, she said, "Mom is going to be pissed when she finds out."

Yeah. True. "Maybe I can say we broke up."

Brandy laughed again. "You're going to have to. But maybe wait a week or two, so she doesn't think you're a pariah."

"Gee, thanks," Everly deadpanned.

It was a joke, but it stung nonetheless and suddenly made Everly wonder what Brock had said about her to Brandy.

"Oh, Everly," Brandy said. "I didn't mean that how it sounded."

"I know," she said. "No worries. It's true that my dating record has been pretty pathetic as of late." Correction: as of forever.

Four

"HAVE A GOOD DAY AT school," Austin told his seven-year-old daughter over the phone.

"Bye, Daddy! Have a good day at work," his daughter said, her sweet voice only making him miss her more.

After hanging up with her, Austin locked up the apartment and headed to the parking lot. His rented apartment had no food, and he hoped there was a café or bakery on the way to the Town office. The town wasn't that big, so locating something wouldn't be too hard, right? Climbing into his truck, he asked Siri for eating establishments. Marshall's Coffee was the first on the list and less than a mile away. Sounded good to Austin.

Moments later, he parked across the street from the coffee shop because the place was pretty crowded. Good to know when the busy hours were in town. He strode across the street. It was still early in the morning, but was already heating up with the June weather. A woman was hurrying along the sidewalk as he walked up to the door so he opened it for her, and she slid past him.

"Oh, thank you," she gushed, her heavily-made-up eyes meeting his gaze. A smile nearly split her face. "And who are you, young man?"

Austin would describe this woman as in her mid-fifties, and she had the vibe of a know-it-all, which proved to be true since he had to stand in line behind her.

"I'm Austin Hayes," he said, wondering if he should shake her hand or something.

"Ah, yes," she said. "I'm Gentry Martin. I work in accounting for the town, so I've seen an invoice or two cross my desk."

She laughed, and he wasn't sure what exactly was funny, but he smiled anyway.

Others in the coffee shop were looking, and Austin guessed it was because he was new in town?

"So, are you single?" Gentry asked. "Married?"

He was surprised at the question, but also not surprised. The woman he'd met last night—Everly—had been direct as well. Although this accountant seemed to be entirely on her own level.

"Who's asking?" he hedged.

The woman laughed again. Loud and high pitched. More heads turned. Not to look at her, but at *him*. Figured.

"I guess I should introduce myself, since I know all about *you*, but you don't know me."

She obviously didn't know all about him since she didn't know his marital status.

"I'm Gentry, like I said," she continued. "I'm fifty-two, divorced, have two Labrador retrievers, both yellow, and I love picnics and nature walks."

Austin literally had no words. Was she reciting her Tinder profile? Not that he'd ever been on Tinder. Okay, so maybe for about twenty minutes a few months ago. But he was off before anything could be considered official.

Gentry was also holding out her hand that was bedecked with no less than six rings. He shook her hand. "Nice to meet you, Ms. Martin."

"Oh, no you don't," she said, gripping his hand. Rather hard. "Everly Falls isn't like that. No formality here. Call me Gentry, please."

Can I have my hand back? was what he wanted to say. "Gentry it is," he said instead, then tugged his hand out of her firm grip.

She poked his bicep. Who did that to a stranger? "So . . . married? Divorced? A handsome guy like you couldn't be single for long."

"Widowed," he said, just to get her to stop with the questions.

Her blue eyes rounded comically. "Oh, my goodness. I'm so, *so* sorry. How long ago did you lose your wife?"

He'd worn a dress shirt today with a tie and everything. Now he was regretting it. The collar was too tight, and the tie felt like it was minutes away from choking him. "A couple of years now." He nodded to the counter they'd been inching toward. "I think it's your turn."

"What can I get you, Gentry?" a man behind the counter asked. He had the name Marshall embroidered on his shirt. His blond hair was either bleached, or this guy spent a lot of time outdoors.

Austin guessed the man to be in his mid-thirties, and he was likely the owner of the joint since his name matched the name of the café.

"Ah, I think I'll have . . ." And what proceeded—which was Gentry making up her mind—took about three full minutes.

No one in line seemed to mind the delay. In fact, when Austin glanced around, the older man in line behind him nodded, and said, "How are you?"

"Good," Austin said. "I'm Austin Hayes, and you are?" Might as well get the introductions over with.

"Yeah, I know," he said, a gleam in his eyes. "I'm Bill Thayer."

"Can I help you?" Marshall said from the counter.

Austin turned to see Marshall smiling at him, his blue eyes curious.

"Welcome to Everly Falls," Marshall continued. "I'm Marshall."

"Austin Hayes."

Marshall's brows lifted. "Any relation to Brock Hayes?"

"Possibly," Austin said. "My dad has cousins here."

Marshall's blond brows lifted. "Ah. You'll have to meet your family then." He grinned. "What'll it be?"

Austin wasn't into the fancy stuff, so he ordered black. "And one of those bagels."

Marshall rang up his purchase while another employee made the coffee, then he handed over a bagel.

Austin turned from the counter and planned to head straight to his truck when he saw a woman walk in—one he recognized.

Her hair was tied up in some sort of scarf this morning, and instead of those red jeans from last night, she wore a black skirt and bright blue blouse. And another pair of heeled sandals—these ones black—although he wasn't really noticing. Just being observant.

Her eyes were green—no, kind of brownish—so, maybe hazel. Last night in the dim lighting of the theater, it was hard to tell. He fully expected her to say hello, but instead, she shifted her gaze from him and took her place in line.

Was she . . . *mad* at him? Truly? He didn't even know the woman, and yet, last night she'd been plenty talkative, despite her announcement of complaining about the renovation.

Her huge bag was up on her shoulder again, and it made him think of the collection of movie stubs she had stashed inside. Which made him feel like smiling.

"Austin," a woman called, and without turning, he knew full well it was Gentry. "Come sit with us."

He glanced over to see Gentry sitting at one of the small, round tables with another woman who had to be in her sixties. Both women's gazes were expectant.

"I've got to head out," he said. "It was nice to meet you."

"Oh." Gentry's entire face fell, then she smiled again.

How did she do that?

"I'll see you soon, then," she called out. Once again, the entire coffee shop had been privy to their conversation.

Everly still hadn't looked over at him, but he had no doubt she'd heard the conversation. He pushed through the door of the coffee shop into the warming air. His suit really was too hot for the middle of June. Once in his truck, he set the coffee in the cup holder, then took a bite of the bagel. Food was good. Food would bring clarity.

The few months spent in this town would be interesting to say the least.

Then he started his truck, but just then Everly stepped out of the coffee shop. No cup in hand. Had she changed her mind? He watched her climb into a small car that she'd parked haphazardly at the curb where there really wasn't room for a parking spot.

Seconds later, she was driving down the street in the same direction he was going.

Austin followed, not surprised when she pulled up to the building that was clearly marked as Town Hall.

Everly was fast, but then again, she wasn't trying to juggle a bagel and coffee.

Austin left half of his uneaten bagel in the truck and

walked into the building, his coffee cup still in hand. He'd entered the building in time to hear Everly's heeled sandals click on the hardwood floor.

She glanced behind her before she pushed open a glass door leading to an office . . . *Mayor Sanders* was inscribed on the glass.

So . . . Everly was going straight to the top, it seemed.

Austin paused and pulled out his phone, looking up the last email he'd received from Town Hall. There it was. Mayor Sanders had been cc'd on all the e-mails. Who knew what Everly was talking to the mayor about? And maybe he didn't have to worry about it.

He'd go with his original idea and visit the planning department to get the blueprints of the theater. The directory by the elevator told him the planning department was on the second floor. He bypassed the elevator and took the stairs up one floor.

There he requested the blueprints from a young man who wouldn't look Austin in the eye. Was the guy nervous or something? When he delivered the blueprints, Austin asked, "Can I take these, or at least take them somewhere to have them copied?"

"I–I don't think so," the young man said.

Austin glanced at the name plate. *Josh.* "What don't you know, Josh? If I can take these or go make a copy?"

Josh shifted his stance, clearly unsure of the answer. "Y–you can take them to have them copied," he said at last. "But bring them back."

Austin was about to ask if there was a place in town where he could get that done when the door behind him opened.

"There you are," a woman said. Gentry again.

Austin knew her voice well by now.

He turned. "Hello, ma'am. Do you know where I can get these blueprints copied?"

"Oh, none of that *ma'am* stuff, Austin," Gentry said, stepping toward him and patting his tie.

Touching him was a bit forward, but she moved away quickly. "Josh, why are you torturing the poor man? Are you hiding the blueprints or something?"

"N–no, Gentry," Josh said, his face fire engine red. "I f– forgot."

Gentry sighed, but it was more good-natured than anything. "Scoot over," she said, walking around the desk. She bent and opened a drawer. A moment later she straightened, a smaller version of the blueprints in her hand.

"Great, thanks," Austin said. "These will help tremendously."

Gentry set her hands on her hips. "I'm good at reading those things if you want any help."

"I'll keep that in mind." Austin moved to the door he'd entered through.

"Don't be a stranger," Gentry said in a cheerful tone. "I can give you a tour of the place if you want."

Austin nodded and reached for the door to pull it open.

"Oh, and by the way, steer clear of Everly," Gentry said, her tone still cheerful as she approached him. "She's as mad as a hornet. You don't know the lengths that Alice went through to keep the renovation under wraps from Everly."

Austin paused at this. "Who's Alice?"

Gentry laughed, then stopped when she saw that his question was sincere. "She's the mayor, of course."

"Right," Austin said. He hadn't known Mayor Sanders's first name until now. "And why was the mayor trying to keep news of the renovation from Everly?"

Gentry took a couple of steps toward him and tapped his tie again. "You'll find out soon enough, dear."

Maybe Austin shouldn't wear a tie next time he came to Town Hall. And *dear*? That was a new one.

"Well, thanks for your help," he said, opening the door this time and escaping. At least it felt like he was escaping. He took the stairs again to the first floor. Walking out of the stairwell, he paused at the sight of the mayor's office.

No sign of Everly through the glass doors. An older woman sat at the reception desk, her graying hair in a tight knot. She wore a red scarf tied about her neck and matching earrings. He wondered if Everly was still inside, talking to Alice Sanders.

Might as well introduce himself.

After opening the glass door, he stepped up to the desk.

Louisa was the name on the name plate. No last name. The woman lifted her green gaze to his. "May I help you, sir?" Her words were casual, yet he was pretty sure she wasn't missing a thing.

"I'm Austin Hayes, the architect hired for the theater renovation," he said. "I thought I'd introduce myself to the mayor . . . that is, if she's in?"

"She's in." Louisa didn't break her gaze as she reached for a desktop phone. Then she pushed a button and said, "Austin Hayes here to see you."

There was a beat of silence, then a crackling voice said, "Thank you, Louisa."

A door behind her swung open, and a woman with graying hair walked out.

Austin guessed her to be in her early sixties. Her brown eyes were warm and lively.

"Austin Hayes, it's wonderful to meet you," she said, extending her hand.

He shook it, then froze. Behind the mayor, Everly hurried out of the office. If Austin wasn't mistaken, she was upset. Everly glanced at him for an instant, then looked away as she strode past. In that instant, he'd seen her distress—her red-rimmed eyes, the tight line of her mouth.

Had she been crying?

She was gone before he could speak to her.

"Come in," Mayor Sanders said. "We need to talk."

Five

It shouldn't matter that she was single, Everly told herself as she walked up the driveway leading to her parents' home. Well, her mother's home now. Her father had passed away years ago, and events like her sister's bridal shower made Everly realize how much her father had missed.

Everly's entire adult life.

The house was lit up against the evening sunset, and laughter and conversation leaked through the door as she stepped onto the porch. For a moment, Everly felt completely separated from the those inside the house. Yes, she was related to a lot of the women who'd be in attendance, but Everly was different.

She'd never married, had never been engaged, hadn't finished college, owned nothing—unless she counted a sketchy car—and her best friend was a stray cat. Oh, not to mention, she had a pretend boyfriend now.

There were worse situations in life to be in. Right?

Everly took a deep breath and opened the door.

Her mom, as usual, had gone all out with decorating. The

living room looked like a glitter bomb had exploded, and silver streamers sparkled along with lavender paper flowers that decorated every available nook.

"Darling," her mother crooned, sweeping forward in one of her perfectly-tailored dresses. "You're late."

Yes, yes, she knew. "Hi, Mom." Everly kissed her mother's cheek.

Then Everly proceeded to greet myriad of aunts, cousins, Brandy's friends, and then finally, her sister Brandy. Her sleek hair looked like it had been salon-styled, and there didn't seem to be a wrinkle on her fitted floral dress anywhere.

"Can we announce your new boyfriend to everyone?" Brandy asked, pulling her into a tight hug.

"Very funny. As you know, it's not exactly announcement material," Everly said. "Plus, this is your party, not mine."

Brandy drew away, a playful pout on her face. "You're such a good sister."

Yes, yes, I am. How many other sisters would be supportive of a boyfriend stealer?

Not that Everly was one to stand in the way of true love. Yet . . .

"So, Tom?" a silky voice spoke into her ear as a cool hand wrapped around her arm.

Everly turned so see Aunt Madge, holding what was probably her third or fourth cocktail. "Your mother swore me to secrecy, but I'm dying for details. I hear he's a lawyer."

Everly felt her face drain of warmth as Madge's acrylic nails dug into her arm. Had Everly embellished her story about Tom? Apparently, she had. "Oh, you know. A very busy lawyer. I don't get to see him as much as I'd like."

"I understand," Marge purred. "My second husband, Bruce, was a lawyer. Bankruptcy. Utterly dull, I'll tell you, but the paycheck was wonderful." Her laugh was low and throaty.

"Um, okay, I should really help with the food in the kitchen." *Please let there be food in the kitchen.* She moved through the crowd of women and arrived in the kitchen. Sure enough, her mother had put together a beautiful spread, likely catered.

Everly perched on a stool and snagged one of the miniature brownies with mint frosting.

The day had started out poorly and hadn't gotten much better after that. Mayor Sanders had assured her that the renovation on the movie theater was locked in, and no one at Town Hall would be changing their minds.

"Why wasn't it put to a vote?" Everly had asked.

"Because it's a renovation, not a new building, or a change in zoning." Mayor Sanders had sighed. "Look Everly, I know that the theater means a lot to you because of your dad. But it doesn't meet the new town codes, and the renovation is a must. I knew if I told you in advance, the approval process could have been delayed."

"What are the plans, then? How much will be renovated?"

The mayor's tone was gentle when she said, "Everything."

And that's when Everly's eyes had burned with tears. Her early memories with her father included going to the movies with him. Mostly it was just her and Dad. Sometimes Brandy and her mother would come, but as Everly got older, Brandy was too busy with her million friends. So Everly and her dad would go. Just them. Get the popcorn. Sit in the middle of the middle. Settle back and escape life for a couple of hours.

Austin the architect had shown up before Everly could ask to see the renovation proposal—if the mayor would even let her see them—so Everly had left.

"Does everyone have a paper and pen?" her mother's

voice rang out from the living room as Everly popped a second bite-sized brownie into her mouth. "Now, write out your best relationship advice to Brandy and Brock. Remember to be honest and not to hold back."

A few giggles and titters came from the living room.

Dear Brandy and Brock, my advice is . . . Nope, she had nothing. But she had to join the women before she was missed and more clucking noises were made.

Quickly, she googled *Marriage Advice for Newlyweds.* A long list popped up, and Everly chose one. She went back to the living room and picked up one of the pink pieces of paper, then wrote: *Never stop being friends.*

Good enough.

And now her stomach hurt. She could blame it on the stolen brownies, but she knew it was because Brock had been *her* friend, her best friend. And perhaps it was losing that friendship that had hurt the most. A person to laugh with, complain to, share the mundane parts of the day with, look forward to seeing . . .

And it wasn't that she couldn't get over a breakup, it was that she was reminded of it every day. Sometimes every minute. She hadn't been allowed to move on because Brock Hayes would be her brother-in-law in a few weeks.

"Oh my gosh, it's absolutely gorgeous," one of her cousin's said, examining Brandy's engagement ring and effectively bringing Everly back to focusing on the party.

"All right, is everyone finished?" Everly's mom said in a brisk tone. "Let's read through them, then time for presents."

Small cheers went up around the room, some of the women raising their already-filled wine glasses. Brandy read through each pink page, smiling, laughing, and finding the advice delightful. Thankfully the advice was all anonymous, and there were a few blushes when the advice turned to bedroom recommendations.

Madge was looking as pleased as the Cheshire cat, so Everly could well guess who'd written that bit of advice.

Then the gift opening commenced. Since Everly's gift was something she and her mom had gone in on together, Brandy opened it first. As she unwrapped the crystal vase and silver picture frame with one of Brandy's engagement photos inside, she grinned. "These will be perfect for our living room. Brock gets me flowers every week anyway, so I'll always have fresh flowers to put in."

Brock used to buy Everly flowers. It seemed he hadn't changed, and that should be a good thing in this case, right?

She hid a sigh and ignored the hollowness forming in her stomach at all the smiles and laughs and general excitement. Everly was happy for her sister, truly. So why did it make her feel more lonely?

Brandy had a bubbly personality, plus she was a drop-dead gorgeous blonde. All the things Everly wasn't. And how *did* Brandy keep her hair so smooth and shiny? Everly was lucky for a day when her hair didn't frizz like it was infused with electricity every moment.

After the guests had finally left, Brandy snagged Everly's hand. She drew her sister into the kitchen where their mom was wrapping up the leftover food that she hadn't been able to send home with their relatives.

"Now, tell us all about Tom," her mom said, glancing over.

Everly wanted to groan, or maybe confess everything to her mom right now. But her mom was watching her with a mixture of excitement and anticipation.

"He's, um, great. You know, really busy and stuff."

"When can we meet him?" her mom asked.

"I know," Brandy said. "How about this Friday? Brock and I are going out to eat. Let's make it a double date, then we can swing by Mom's and make introductions."

"Uh—" Yeah, Everly didn't know whether to laugh hysterically or strangle her sister.

"Perfect," her mom cut in. "I could have dessert ready."

Everly shot Brandy a dagger-glare. "I'll have him check his schedule."

"No courts of law are open on Friday night," Brandy countered with a laugh.

Everly fake-laughed in return. "I know, but he's got all those cases to review."

Her mother frowned. "What type of law does he practice?"

Everly froze, her gaze flitting about the kitchen. *Come on brain, work.*

"Didn't you tell me family law?" Brandy asked in a completely innocent tone.

"He's a *divorce* attorney?" Her mother's brows shot up.

"Yep." Everly's voice sounded very, very small. She shot her sister a look that said, *Stop talking about my fake boyfriend.*

Brandy just gave her an innocent look. Then her phone buzzed, distracting her. "Oh, Brock's coming over. He's going to love all the gifts I got."

Time to leave. "I forgot I have a thing tonight," Everly said. "I told my boss I'd update the website for her." It was true, but she didn't have to do it tonight. Everly snatched her purse from the corner of the kitchen counter. "Thanks for the yummy food, Mom. And see you both soon."

Just like that, she was out the door and striding to her car. Away from any more potential questions from her mom, and Brandy egging it on.

Everly drove slowly down the street, arguing with herself. She should have never told her mom she was dating someone. Just because her mom was obsessive about Everly's love life, didn't mean she had to inflate and create something out of nothing.

Besides, Mr. Wonderful would come around someday. And until then, she'd be content and worry free from problematic relationships.

Her car seemed to slow on its own as she drove past the theater. The final movie of the night was long over, but there were lights on inside. And a vehicle in the parking lot. A white truck to be exact.

Huh.

Austin Hayes must be inside. Strategizing how he was going to demolish her childhood memories.

Everly pulled over to the side of the road and sat for a moment, gazing at the place she'd loved for so long. The place she never thought would change. Not in her small town.

Before she knew it, she'd opened her door and climbed out. She had successfully avoided talking to Austin Hayes that day so far, so why was she now walking toward the theater? Maybe she could talk him out of making too many changes. But who was she kidding? Austin Hayes was an architect, and he'd do his job, then leave Everly Falls forever. He wouldn't care about the sentimentalities of a woman he didn't even know.

The theater door was locked, and after peering inside, she couldn't see Austin anyway. Had he gone through one of the back doors? She walked around the building and found the door closest to where he'd parked. Ah-ha. It was unlocked, and yes, she should have second-guessed her actions, but instead, she walked right in. The dim hallway led to office space behind the theater rooms. But he wasn't there.

He wasn't in the lobby either.

She peeked into one theater room to find it pitch dark. So, she headed to the second theater.

"The theater's closed," a deep voice said behind her.

She let out a small yelp, then turned, her hand on her chest. "Oh, you scared me."

Austin Hayes stood there with an eyebrow raised. He wasn't wearing a jacket or a dress shirt and tie. No, he wore an off-white t-shirt that had seen better days and some ratty looking jeans that fit him perfectly, looking like heaven to her.

"What are you doing?" she asked.

His brow remained lifted. "I should ask that of you. Do you make it a habit of coming into closed buildings at night?"

"No." She inhaled. Exhaled. Austin Hayes smelled rather nice in this close proximity. Maybe a shaving cream? Something subtle and woodsy. "I saw the lights and the truck and wanted to ask you some questions."

He gazed at her for a second, brown eyes steady on hers. "Sure," he said at last.

She couldn't explain the relief that shot through her. Glancing at the iPad in his hand, she asked, "Do you have your proposal on there?"

Two faint lines appeared between his brows. "My proposal?"

"You know, for the renovation." She took a small step back and put a bit of distance between herself and his wonderful scent—some sort of spicy soap? She might have also taken an accidental peek at his hand—left hand. No wedding ring, but that didn't always signify a man's marital status.

"The town hired our company because of my dad's connection to Everly Falls," he said. "I didn't submit a proposal. The town called us."

"Oh." This she hadn't considered. "What are their plans, then?"

The edges of his mouth lifted. "Why are you so interested, Everly? Did you used to work here?"

He'd remembered her name, and a small thrill buzzed her skin. Maybe she should reactivate her dating app, because here she was, feeling flattered when an out-of-town stranger knew her name. A handsome stranger, true, but still, unless she wanted to move out of town, any interest in a man living elsewhere had to be squashed immediately.

And . . . he was waiting for an answer.

Six

THIS WOMAN WAS INTRIGUING TO say the least, and she still wasn't answering his question. Although, it was good news that Everly was no longer avoiding him like she had that morning. And she wasn't crying. She'd changed again and wore light orange pants with a white V-neck shirt. She wore plenty of bracelets again, and her hair was tamer than he'd seen it. Oh, her dark blonde curls were still pretty wild, but her hair was pulled back from her face. A few tendrils lay against her neck, and Austin wondered if her hair felt as soft as it looked.

He was about to repeat his question when she said, "I did work here once, but that's not why I love the place. My dad used to bring me here as a kid."

Ah. So, personal it was.

"This theater was kind of our hangout." She shrugged and looked down. "He's been gone for several years, but I still come here a lot. Nostalgic, I guess."

When she met his gaze, he saw the pain in the depths of her eyes. Pain that he was intimately familiar with.

When Austin had heard someone else in the theater, he hadn't exactly been alarmed. He thought maybe the janitor had forgotten something. He'd spent the better part of the day reviewing the blueprints, then calling his crew to talk about materials and timing. He'd need to make final decisions by tomorrow to get everything ordered and delivered. The following day, his crew would arrive to begin the work.

Finally, after he'd grabbed some dinner and wrapped up all of his phone calls and emails, he had headed to the theater as it was closing down for the night. He'd been intent on walking the entire interior and making notes. He had an idea of how to keep the theater up and running during renovation. He just hoped the town would go for it since it would now take a few extra weeks.

Not that he wanted to be away from his daughter any longer, but maybe he could work in a couple of weekend visits back home.

"What was your dad's name?" he asked Everly.

She looked surprised at this. "Bruce."

Austin nodded. "What did Bruce Kane like about the theater?"

At this, she smiled, and Austin decided he liked her smile much better than her tears.

"Everything," she said. "I mean, the excitement of a night out is probably the first thing. The snacks—he was a popcorn nut. And well, me, I guess. Daddy daughter dates. And of course, being transported into another world for a couple of hours."

Austin leaned against the opposite wall from her. "What did he like about this building?"

Her gaze scanned the hallway. "He never said specifically, but when I was a kid, he'd point out the arches and the detail work above them. Said they were like tiny book scrolls since a lot of movies were stories first."

"We can preserve that kind of stuff."

Her hazel eyes widened. "You can?"

"Sure," he said. "I might have to get creative since the town already sent me their proposal, but I can talk to them about adjustments."

The relief that crossed her face filled Austin with warmth. "That would be amazing. I thought that you'd start from scratch."

"No," Austin said. "Is that what the mayor told you?"

"She told me that they had no choice but to renovate since the building was violating some safety codes," Everly said. "So, I guess I pictured a demolition."

The edges of his mouth lifted, but he didn't want to laugh, because he could see that her distress had been real. "No demolition."

"No?" She was grinning now. "What are the basic plans?"

He loved that she was smiling, and he loved that her whole demeanor had brightened. "Well, the structure is sound, but the wiring and sound system needs to be completely replaced," he said. "The town wants new chairs and carpet, and we'll have to upgrade concessions."

"No more smells of burnt popcorn and grease?" she asked.

He chuckled. "Don't tell me you'll miss that too?"

"I think I will," she said with a smirk. "What about the rest?"

"How about I show you?" He nodded toward the door leading into one of the theaters. This would of course prolong their conversation, but Austin found he was rather enjoying time spent with this woman. It had been a long time since he'd had a conversation with a woman where there hadn't been some sort of expectation of a relationship.

This was no date, no expectation of any kind, and he liked that.

"All right, I guess I have a few minutes."

Austin did smile then, but she'd already turned and was walking toward the theater. *She* was the one who'd come into the theater after hours, of course she had time.

Austin caught up with her and opened the theater door before she could reach it. She passed by him, and yep, there was that subtle flowery scent of hers.

For a moment, they were surrounded by complete blackness until he found the switch plate for the lights and turned them up as high as they'd go.

Being in the empty theater again with her reminded him of the night before when she'd awakened him.

"The architecture in here is basically a hodgepodge," he said as they walked along the aisle. "I'm going to fix that."

She glanced at him. "How long have you been an architect? And did you always want to be one? You said you worked for your dad?" Her face flushed a pretty pink. "Sorry, lots of questions."

Austin found he didn't mind. He also had questions. Like how old was she? And was she in a relationship? She didn't wear a wedding ring amongst all of her other jewelry.

"I took an architecture class in high school, and I fell in love with it. I was already a doodler, so expanding that wasn't too much of an effort."

Everly's brows drew together. "I'm sure it took plenty of effort."

"Oh, yeah, well, college did, but I love the work." He shrugged. "Now architecture is only part of my job. My dad's construction business specializes in renovations, so when I started working for him, I wore many hats. He's in recovery now from a surgery, otherwise I probably wouldn't have been so involved in this project, since he was looking forward to coming to Everly Falls."

She started to move again, walking along a row, with her hand trailing the edges of the theater chairs. "How long will it take?"

"That's what I'm trying to determine." He watched her turn and move into the next row. "I'd like to close only one theater room down at a time, then one theater could stay in operation."

"Oh, wow." She stopped. "That would be amazing."

"Yeah?"

Her smile bloomed. "Yeah."

Was she blushing again? Austin tried to remember the last woman who'd blushed around him. Rachel? He honestly couldn't remember.

A phone rang, and they both checked their pockets. Everly held hers up. "It's me." Then her brow furrowed when she looked at the screen. "I should take this."

She turned around and answered. "No, Mom, I'm still awake. You know me, I'm a night owl . . . Um, I haven't had the chance to ask him yet."

Austin probably shouldn't be eavesdropping, but there was literally no other person or distraction around. He was also curious about her pensive tone. Were things okay with her mom? Yet, it sounded like they were discussing a guy. Maybe Everly's boyfriend?

Austin couldn't explain why that made him feel antsy. He'd barely met Everly, and yeah, he was enjoying talking to her and he found her interesting. But a lot of women were interesting, right? And beautiful. Everly happened to be both.

Everly sat in the nearest chair with a sigh. "I will as soon as I can," she said, her tone now resigned. "He's so busy though, so I don't want you to get your hopes up . . . Oh, that's nice. Say hi to, um, Brock for me . . . Yes, I'm fine. It is late, so maybe I sound tired, but I'm fine . . . Okay, Mom, talk to you later."

She hung up then and buried her face in her hands with a groan.

Austin stilled. Was she upset? Crying?

He didn't move, not wanting to intrude. Maybe she'd forgotten he was here, and maybe he'd overheard some personal stuff. Although it had been impossible to decipher.

"Have you ever done something really stupid?" she mumbled.

Austin blinked. She was talking to him, at least he thought she was, even though her face was still buried in her hands.

He perched against the back of the chair he was next to, which put them about three rows apart. "I have."

Everly lifted her head, and he was glad she wasn't crying at least. She only looked perplexed and maybe annoyed. At her mother? At whoever they'd been discussing?

"Like what?" Everly asked.

This caught Austin off-guard. "Um . . ." He knew the answer, but it was kind of personal. "When my wife told me she was going to stay a few nights a week at her friend's place to be closer to her job and cut back on commuting, I agreed."

Everly blinked, but she was focused on him.

Yeah, probably not what she expected to hear. "I agreed," he repeated, "and I regret that. She was diagnosed soon after with cancer, and I think if I'd been around her more, I might have noticed her symptoms. Could have gotten her to the doctor sooner. Maybe she wouldn't have died."

Everly covered her mouth with her hand in a gasp. Then she blinked rapidly and lowered her hand. "I'm really sorry, Austin. I had no idea, and I didn't mean—"

"It's okay," he said. "I've done a lot of stupid things, but that tops them all."

Their conversation had gone to one-hundred-percent personal in about three seconds flat.

"You can't blame yourself for your wife's cancer," she said in a soft voice.

"I know," he said. "But the *what ifs* still plague me."

She didn't speak for a moment, then she stood from the chair and walked down the row away from him. At the end of the row, she turned and walked into his row. She stopped a few feet from him, her hazel gaze on his. "I'm the queen of *what ifs*. I mean, my sister is marrying my ex-boyfriend in a few weeks, and to cope with it all and keep everyone from feeling sorry for me, I made up a guy I'm dating."

Austin stared at her.

"And get this," she continued. "Under pressure, I told them his name was Tom Middleston."

His mouth twitched. "They believed you?"

"Completely," Everly said. "My sister and her fiancé, who is probably related to you by the way since his last name is Hayes, invited me on a double date in order to meet Tom."

Austin smiled.

"It's not funny."

A laugh escaped him. "It's a little funny."

Her lips curved. "Maybe a little funny, but now I'll have to go through a fake breakup. A real breakup is hard enough." Her eyes rounded. "Of course, I'm not complaining, I mean, you're dealing with real tragedy."

Austin's smile didn't diminish though. "I'm sure we could spend all day comparing our sad lives, but maybe we could do it over food somewhere? I'm starving."

Everly opened her mouth, then shut it. She was definitely blushing.

"Or . . . not," he said. "Would Tom be upset?"

She blushed even more. "Um, it's kind of late. For a small town." She glanced at her cell phone. "Every place closes by eight or nine on a week night."

He straightened. He'd crossed the line. Big time. "Good to know. I'll have to grocery shop then, maybe keep my place better stocked."

Everly smoothed back some of her hair. He'd made her nervous, and that bothered him. He didn't want her to be nervous around him. "The grocery store is closed too."

He nodded. Figured. He probably had some granola bars in his truck.

"But I could make you something," she said quickly. "At my place. It will be simple since I don't have a full kitchen, but it would be better than going to bed hungry."

He held her gaze for a second. Was she just being nice, or was she sincere in her offer? Because he really was hungry, and well, he wouldn't mind spending more time with her. Still, he hesitated.

"I have a cat," she said with a slight wince. "Only one, though. I'm not a cat lady or anything . . . I'm not that pathetic, but I thought I should let you know in case you're allergic."

"I'm not allergic."

Her smile was tentative as she again smoothed back her hair. "Okay, then, whatever you want to do. I don't think Tom would mind. He's never around."

Austin laughed, and Everly grinned.

"Okay, I'd like to see more of your town anyway."

Seven

WHAT HAD SHE BEEN THINKING? Inviting Austin Hayes to her
dumpy little apartment above the craft store of all places? This
good-looking, well-dressed guy with an amazing career as a
professional architect and a previous wife who'd probably
been sophisticated and gorgeous would certainly get a kick out
of her tiny box of a home.

And of all things, Everly had offered to *cook* for him. She
was not the greatest cook. Yes, she could make a dozen or so
things decently, but had she ever cooked for Brock? She
honestly couldn't remember. If she had then it had been
utterly unremarkable.

Yet, here Everly was, pulling into the parking lot behind
the craft store with Austin's white truck rumbling behind her.
She parked, then climbed out of her car. And there *he* was.
Climbing out of his truck. This was really happening.

"This way," she called in a voice that she hoped sounded
nonchalant, yet was tinged with nervous energy.

She was being a good neighbor. He was a widower, for
crying out loud. A man who'd been married to the love of his

life. A tragic hero who was in a new town, away from home, and had no food at his place. Big deal if she made him scrambled eggs and toast. He'd be appreciative, right?

Of course, he would. Austin Hayes was proving to be a decent guy. One who really listened to her. Offered compromises about her beloved theater and hadn't been put off by her personality yet.

And . . . the lock to the back door of the shop was stuck. She rattled her key in the lock, then tried again. Nope. Nothing. "Hang on," she said, pulling out her key, then sticking it back into the lock again.

On the odd day, the lock wouldn't turn for whatever reason. Her boss had told her more than once that she'd get it replaced. Well, that day hadn't been today.

She glanced at him. "Sorry, it gets stuck sometimes." This close up, his eyes were dark brown beneath the light over the back door. His clean spice scent was as she remembered it. Nice. She tugged her gaze from appreciating how his t-shirt pulled across his chest and emphasized the broadness of his shoulders.

She stuck the key into the lock again. Maybe this had all been a bad idea.

"Can I try?" Austin said after Everly had attempted pulling out the key and putting it back in about eight times.

"Sure." She handed him the key and moved back.

Austin stuck the key in, wiggled it a bit, then turned it again. The door unlocked.

Her mouth fell open. "How did you do that?"

Austin flashed her a smile. "I was a latchkey kid, and my parents' back door was as stubborn as a mule."

"Huh," she said. He had a really great smile, but she wouldn't let it affect her. The last thing she needed to be doing was acting like she'd never invited a man up to her place.

Brock had been there a few times, but they'd normally hung out at his place.

Austin pushed open the door and motioned for her to go ahead of him.

She walked into the shop. The night lights glowed just enough to lead the way to the stairwell and the door that said *Do Not Enter.*

"I'm up here," she said, then looked behind her.

Austin had stopped, his hands on his hips, looking around the place.

"Pretty great, huh?" she said. And it was. The craft store was pristinely organized, with about every knickknack a crafter could want.

"There's so much stuff," he said, his voice filled with awe. "How do the customers find anything?"

Everly smiled. "Simple. The aisles are organized by type of craft. We have a sewing aisle, photo album aisle, stampers aisle, needlepoint aisle, and that's just to start."

"Wow."

Meow.

Snatches was hungry too.

Austin turned to her. "Is that your non-cat-lady cat?"

"It is." Everly opened the staircase door and flipped on the light. "She's waiting for her dinner."

"Then by all means, let's eat."

Everly laughed and headed up the stairs. Austin followed her, and she could only hope that she'd made her bed that morning and straightened things up. From her perch at the top of the steps, Snatches took one look at Austin and darted away.

"Sorry, she might be afraid of you," Everly said.

They reached the landing, and Everly waved toward the room beyond. It was divided into a kitchen area, sitting area, and bedroom. Sort of.

"Have a seat," Everly said. "I'll find something to cook up." She wasn't entirely sure what she'd make, but hopefully he wasn't picky.

Austin didn't sit on the loveseat or at the half-sized kitchen table. Instead, he wandered around the living space.

Everly tried not to let it bother her that he was scrutinizing her art, which hung in frames on the walls. If he said he didn't like it, maybe she'd tell him she'd bought it somewhere, although that was now impossible because he'd leaned forward to read the artist's name in the corner. Hers.

"You must like old movies?" he said after a moment.

Yeah, the art canvases were portraits of movie stars from eras before. No one modern. Portraits of Greta Garbo, Gloria Swanson, Rudolph Valentino, and other 1920s and 1930s film icons.

"I do, in fact," she said, checking on the lettuce in her fridge. It still looked good, and she still had the ground meat she'd bought last weekend and put in the freezer after cooking it up. "Does taco salad sound okay?"

She turned to find Austin only a few feet from her.

"You're a talented artist," he said, his brown eyes on hers.

"Are you an art connoisseur or something?" she teased because his compliment was making her feel warm.

"Do I have to be?" he asked, the edge of his mouth lifting. "Can I like something without comparing it?"

Her own smile grew. "You can." Then she shrugged. "I don't paint anymore. Those are all from my failed year at college. Instead of studying for my tests, I got on a huge kick of painting retro actors."

"And the result is on your walls?"

"Correct."

Austin was studying her like he was trying to figure her out. "Why don't you paint anymore?"

"Gotta pay the bills," she said as nonchalantly as she could. That was only part of the reason. When Brock had seen her work, he'd asked if being a copy artist was legal. As in, he thought everything she painted should have been original. But it wasn't only that. She had entered multiple art contests and never received any sort of recognition.

"Then pay the bills," Austin said, his voice low. "But don't give up what you love."

His comment surprised her. So opposite of Brock, not that she was comparing. Okay, so she was.

"Well, I don't have to deal with rejection anymore," she said. "I used to try to get into the local art galleries, but never did. One year I set up a booth to sell my work at the Town art fair. Sold two pieces—both to my mom."

"Your mom has good taste then."

"You're sweet," she said. She might also be blushing again. "But the door's closed on my angsty past."

His gaze was thoughtful, then he looked past her to the counter. "I can help."

"It's okay," she said. "It won't take long. The meat is precooked."

He moved to the sink and turned on the water. Then he began washing his hands.

All right, then . . .

"Give me a job," he said, his smile something she found hard to turn down. "I'm not going to sit around while you're cooking dinner."

So, he tore up the lettuce and chopped a couple of tomatoes while she warmed up the meat and assembled the rest of the ingredients.

Snatches came out from under the bed as the meat was warming up and jumped onto the table, her shyness long forgotten.

"Hey there," Austin said. "I think she wants what we're having."

Everly scooped up the cat. "You know you're not supposed to be on the table." With one hand, she got the cat's food ready, then set Snatches in front of it.

She ate, but kept an ear tuned to the rest of the dinner preparations.

Everly wanted to pinch herself for the fact that a man was in her apartment and they were making dinner together. Not that she could tell anyone, especially her mom who thought she was dating Tom Middleston.

She stroked Snatches for a moment while watching the real man in her kitchen pull down plates from one of the two cupboards she had.

"Am I setting the table for two or three?" Austin asked.

"Two," Everly said. "Snatches will have to mind her manners."

"Snatches, huh?" Austin looked over at her, his brown eyes amused.

So, as they finished setting the table, Everly told Austin of the cat's sudden appearance.

"And you've been best friends ever since?" he said as they sat down at the table, both with plates piled with taco salad.

Everly considered his question. "Well, I do tell her a lot of things, and she does keep all of my secrets. Does that make me pathetic to say *yes?*"

"No, I get it," Austin said. "I had a dog as a kid, and he was definitely my best friend." He started to eat, so Everly did too.

"This is great, thank you," he said after a couple of bites

She shrugged. "It's easy."

Meow.

"Don't you dare—"

But it was too late. Austin had given Snatches a bite of his meat. The cat promptly jumped into his lap and began to purr as she sniffed around for more.

"She likes it," he said, looking at Everly with an innocent expression.

"Of course, she does, but now she'll get into a bad habit of begging for food."

Austin chuckled while he patted the cat's head then set her down.

Everly had to smile at that because her cat was obviously smitten with the man. Not that she could argue with the animal's taste in humans.

They continued eating, and Austin slipped meat to Snatches a couple more times, which made Everly laugh. When she rose to clear the table and do the dishes, Austin stood too.

"I can do that," he said, reaching for the plate in her hand.

But she nudged him to the side and walked to the kitchen sink. "You're my guest, Austin Hayes," she said. "You helped me cook, you don't have to clean up."

He sidled next to her at the sink and washed out their drinking glasses. "I'll wash, you dry. See, it goes faster with help."

"Are you in a hurry?" she asked, then hoped she hadn't sounded too flirty.

"I'm not in a hurry," he said, his voice low. "I also don't want to intrude."

They weren't touching, but it was like she could feel the heat of him. She watched his hands making quick work of washing the dishes, so she used a dish towel to start drying them.

She looked up at him as he turned off the water. His brown eyes held hers, and she swallowed against her suddenly-dry throat. "You're not intruding."

Was he leaning closer? Had his eyes just dipped to her mouth? *Don't panic, Everly. Breathe.*

His hand brushed hers, and she thought surely, he was going to pull her close. But no, he took the dishcloth from her hands and dried his own hands.

Why was she feeling disappointed? It wasn't like she could expect him to sweep her in his arms and kiss her or anything. Just because she too easily fantasized, didn't mean he did. No, Austin Hayes was a perfectly level-headed man.

"What else is there to do in this small town?" he asked, using the damp towel to wipe down her single counter top.

She knew it was futile to tell him he didn't have to keep cleaning. "Well, if you like hiking, Everly Falls is perfect for that," she said. "But if you like beaches, we're about a half day's drive from one. Do you surf or anything?" She could imagine him a surfer in his younger days, and perhaps he still did.

He looked over at her, his mouth quirked. "No. I don't surf. I grew up more inland, and my family rarely did beach stuff."

She nodded. "What about sports?"

"Basketball in high school."

She wasn't surprised he played sports. "Were you any good?"

He leaned against the counter and folded his arms, studying her. "I was decent. Wasn't good enough for college, but I could hold my own in high school. What about you? Any high school sports?"

His brown eyes were full humor. Was he mocking her?

She obviously didn't have the height or body type for any type of sport. "Um, I was more of an art geek."

His brows rose, the smile still in those warm brown eyes. "Are artists geeks?"

"Compared to jocks they are."

54

"Can't say I've known any artists, so I'll have to get back to you on that assessment," he said. "Besides, architecture has some similarities to art, right?"

Snatches rubbed against her legs, practically begging to be picked up. Everly obliged and held the cat close. "I think architecture is a lot more analytical than randomly painting something. But maybe that means you're part geek, part jock."

He chuckled. "I hated high school labels."

"Me too." She was pretty much smiling stupidly at him. She should be playing it cool, as if her skin wasn't humming and her pulse wasn't skipping ahead.

"What else does your town have?"

She wondered why he was so interested, but for the sake of conversation, she said, "We have a small amusement park, but it's overrun with teens. The typical mall, one golf course, and a mini golf course—more teens abound there. Otherwise, places to eat like a burger joint, a pizza place, you know, all the standard stuff. Oh, and several of the hikes lead to waterfalls. One of them has a great swimming hole, although I haven't been up there for a while."

"We should check it out then."

Had he just . . . invited her someplace? "Oh, uh, that might be fun."

His gaze hadn't moved from hers. "You don't sound too excited."

"I'm . . . surprised at the suggestion is all." She bit her lip, silently telling herself to stop talking. But she kept rambling anyway because that's apparently what she did around this hunky man with gorgeous brown eyes. "I didn't think you'd want to hang out with me more than . . . now? I mean, you don't owe my anything if that's what you're thinking. Dinner's on me tonight, good neighbor stuff, and all." Was her face red? She was pretty sure the answer was *yes*.

His brown gaze remained steady as if he was perfectly willing to let her dig her own hole deeper and deeper. "Is it Tom?" he asked, his mouth quirking at the corners. "Or is there a real boyfriend you haven't told me about?"

She rolled her eyes. "No boyfriend. As if."

His brows lifted, and she supposed she had to explain herself.

"I haven't dated anyone more than a single date since Brock, uh, dumped me." She set down Snatches because the cat was getting antsy. The cat promptly walked over to Austin and proceeded to nudge his legs. "Small towns are sort of hard to start a new relationship in. Everyone knows me, and I know everyone. The moment I show up somewhere with a guy, the news spreads to my mom and sister."

"No privacy, huh?" he asked. "I think I got a dose of that with Gentry earlier today."

Everly shook her head. "Yeah, watch out or Gentry will eat *you* for dinner."

"She's got to be in her fifties," he said.

"Oh, she's not picky."

Austin laughed, and Everly grinned.

"So, if we go on a hike, then you're saying the whole town will know about it?"

Everly felt like a hoard of butterflies had awakened in her belly. "Yep."

"I have no problem with that, do you?"

She sighed with exaggeration to cover up what was sure to be another blush. "I'm going to have to break up with Tom first, because I don't want him to think I'm two-timing him."

Austin's expression was perfectly straight when he said, "Let me know when you do."

Eight

Once in a while, a full day would pass, and Austin would realize he hadn't thought of Rachel at all. Today had been one of those days. It wasn't until he called Jessica before her bedtime that Rachel even crossed his mind.

"What are you doing, Daddy?" Jessica asked, her sweet voice coming through the phone.

"Well, I'm cleaning up after dinner," he said. "How was summer camp today?"

"Okay. I found a frog."

"Really? What kind of frog?"

"I don't know," Jessica said with a sigh. "My friend Caleb said it was going to bite me. But do frogs have teeth?"

Austin had to think about that for a second. "I don't think so," he said. "Where did you see the frog?"

"By the trees."

He smiled. It wasn't like he'd get a ton of details out of a seven-year-old. "What did you have for dinner tonight?"

"Macaroni and cheese, then Grandma made me eat carrots."

"They're good for you," Austin said.

"That's what Grandma said." She sighed again. "When are you coming home?"

"Well, I'll be home in about a week for a visit," he said. "But I have to come back here and work some more."

"Can I come with you?" she asked, her tone brightening.

"Not this time, sweetheart," Austin said. "I don't have a bed for you, and I'm working very long days in order to get the job done sooner."

"Okay, Daddy." Another sigh.

He hated being away from her for long stretches. "I love you."

"I love you more."

Austin chuckled. "I love you more."

This was their thing every night at bedtime, and Austin wouldn't trade it for the world. They'd began it when Rachel had started staying in the city . . . with her boyfriend, apparently. And now, Austin was thinking of his wife. Bittersweet because he couldn't even be mad at her—she'd taken that from him too.

But today had been different from many other days previous because his thoughts had been preoccupied all day with another woman. *Everly.* Last night's dinner at her place had been impromptu and surprisingly fun. He hadn't known exactly what to think when she told him she'd made up a boyfriend to get out of all the sympathy comments leading up to her sister's wedding, but it sort of fit her quirky personality.

He'd left her apartment much later than he'd expected to. They'd talked late into the night about random stuff he'd never really discussed with anyone before. Or felt the need to. With Everly, it was different. Talking to her was easy. He'd told her all about Jessica and how he was already missing her. They talked about their childhoods, of all things. Everly laughed at his stories of his childhood, and he laughed at hers. Maybe too much.

At one point she slugged him in the arm, and he'd grabbed her hand and said, "Careful, or I might think you like me."

She'd blushed then. A pretty pink.

At that moment, he realized he liked Everly. Well, he knew he liked her, but he liked her in a way that he hadn't expected. He wanted to see her again. It was too late tonight, but maybe he could text her? They hadn't firmed up any plans to do something like go on a hike, but she hadn't exactly turned him down either.

Austin sat on the edge of his bed, second guessing himself. He'd only be in Everly Falls for a couple of months. Dating a local woman probably wasn't the best idea. He wasn't looking for a fling, yet, he wasn't looking for a commitment either. Having a daughter made dating seem very complicated.

Was he interested in Everly above other women because she was conveniently here? Because his life as a dad felt at a distance when he could only talk to his daughter on the phone? Dating a woman closer to home would involve so much more, and Jessica would be a part of that relationship too.

But here, in Everly Falls, Jessica wouldn't even have to meet someone he dated. There'd be no disruption in her life as far as her dad bringing a new woman around.

Austin exhaled. His intentions toward Everly were . . . what? Friendly, he decided. He could have friends in this town, and one of them could be an interesting, beautiful single woman. Right?

It wasn't like he was a player or a heartbreaker. If anything, his heart had been broken by his wife. Sometimes he wondered what would have happened to their marriage if Austin had found out about her affair before she got sick. Would they have split up?

The short answer was yes, but the long answer was murky. What if she'd apologized and asked for forgiveness? Austin knew he would have done almost anything to keep their family together. In the end, though, even forgiveness wouldn't have been enough. Rachel had left them both permanently.

He could text Everly. See where it led. One step. That was all.

See any great movies lately?

Austin groaned when he realized it was after 11:00 pm. Even if she was a night owl, it wasn't polite to text so late. Hopefully she turned her phone off at night. He set his phone on the bedside table, then changed for the night. By the time he settled into bed, Everly had texted back.

The Avengers was great. You should see it sometime.

Austin smiled. First, because she'd replied, and second, there was a hint of flirtation in her response. *Haha,* he wrote. *I heard it puts grown men to sleep.*

She sent a smiling emoji.

His heart thumped once, twice, then he wrote: *Can I call you?* Texting was fine for short communication, but he'd rather talk to Everly. Hear her voice and figure out why he hadn't been able to get her off his mind. Maybe it had been a fluke. Or maybe not.

Okay.

He pressed send on her number, and she answered on the second ring.

"Hi."

Austin smiled at the sound of her voice. "Hi. Is it too late to call?"

"It's too late to ask since you already did," she said.

He laughed. "Good point."

"Long day working?"

"Yeah, that's a good way to put it," he said. "But most of the orders are put in, and my crew arrives tomorrow morning."

"Wow, it's moving fast," she said, her tone sounding wistful.

"It will look great, don't worry," he said. "You can even come visit the job site if you want to see how things are progressing. You know, in between your job and your movie schedule, which will be limited now."

"I saw the new hours posted on the theater website," she said. "I'll have to make some major adjustments. I mean, the single theater will now be more crowded if there's only one option, and I like my special seat, you know."

"I know," he said. "I might have to fight you for it."

She laughed, and that only made his smile grow. "I have no problem coming early to the theater to get my seat."

"Except I'll be there all day, and as soon as I see your car pull up, I can beat you to it."

She scoffed. "You wouldn't dare."

"You're right," he said. "I'd be the gentleman and defer to you."

"And I would let you."

He was grinning. Like a fool. "So, the weather is supposed to be decent this weekend. I thought maybe you should take me on one of those hikes you told me about."

"Oh, you think *I* should take *you*?" she teased.

"If you want," he said. "I mean, I wouldn't be opposed if you asked me."

She laughed.

And he was still grinning. "Okay, if you insist on being

old-fashioned, then I'll ask you. And I'll pick you up. I'll even pay for our meal, or two, depending on how long all the hiking takes."

"Hmm."

"Is that a yes or no?"

"I'm working Saturday, and on Sunday, my sister asked me to come to a brunch with her almost in-laws."

Austin paused. "As in the in-laws that might have been yours if you and Brock hadn't broken up?"

"Possibly?"

"Well, I think you need to tell your sister that you have other plans," he said.

"You do?"

"I do," he said in a firm tone. "Unless you really want to go to that brunch."

"I don't, in fact," she said. "You know how family puts on the pressure though, right?"

"Right . . . the kind of pressure that leads you to making up a boyfriend? That kind of pressure?" Maybe he'd gone too far, but he couldn't imagine agreeing to such a brunch.

Everly was quiet for a moment. Then she said, "What time can you pick me up?"

He was back to smiling. "Does eleven work?"

"Perfect."

And just like that, he had a date.

Sunday couldn't come fast enough, and by Saturday morning, he was feeling as jittery as a high school kid waiting for his first prom. So, on his lunch break, he decided to drop by the craft store. He probably had to buy something there, right?

"Jimmy," Austin said, walking up to his foreman on the job. The past few days, the crew had mostly been tearing out the old carpet and seats in the first theater room. The renovations on the concessions would start next week.

Jimmy Arnold had been working for Austin's dad as long as he could remember. The guy was sixty-five, completely bald, but still spry. In fact, he had more energy than most of the younger crew members.

"What's up, boss?" Jimmy asked.

"I'm heading to the craft store in town, is there anything you need me to pick up?"

Jimmy rubbed the back of his neck. "At a craft store? I don't think so, boss. But lunch would be nice."

Austin chuckled. "Got it. I'll be back soon."

On his drive over, he scoured his brain over what he might pick up at the craft store. Wood glue? Good enough.

He parked down the block from the craft store since there seemed to be some sort of summer sale going on, and the place was busy. Would the place be too busy for him to have a chance to talk to Everly? Hopefully it wasn't, and they could talk for a minute.

Austin walked along the sidewalk, enjoying the chance to be outside in the middle of the day. The day was warm, the humidity was down, so it was all quite pleasant.

He stepped into the craft store, and it didn't take long for him to spot Everly. She was ringing up the line of waiting customers. So, he decided to browse for a few minutes to see if the line would go down soon.

Everly was wearing a green summer dress, and her hair was in a side-braid that rested over her shoulder. She laughed at something a customer said, and the sound of her laughter warmed Austin even though he wasn't the recipient.

He moved down the aisle so he wouldn't be caught ogling, but he couldn't help glancing over a time or two as the line moved forward. Wandering to the back of the store, he picked up a bottle of wood glue as someone said, "Can I help you?"

He turned to see an older woman, wearing a shirt embroidered with *Darla's Crafts* on it.

"I found what I needed," he said, holding up the wood glue.

"Those are on sale, you know, buy one get one half off."

"Oh," he said. "I should get two then."

"What else are you looking for?" she asked, her dark brown eyes peering at him, reminding him of Gentry from the Town Hall.

"I'm just looking around," he said.

She nodded. "Are you new in town?"

"Sort of," he said, then explained about the theater.

"Oh yes, I've heard of you then," the woman said. "You're Austin Hayes, right?"

"Right."

"Darla Brown." She tilted her head. "I guess you're wanting to talk to Everly? She told me all about you."

Austin couldn't have been more surprised. "She did?"

Darla nodded with a knowing gleam in her eye. "I'll let her know you're here."

"Okay," Austin said, his mind still spinning. What had Everly said about him to her boss? He moved to the next aisle and stopped when he saw a display of what looked like the same type of art in Everly's apartment. They were prints though, and not original paintings. He leaned in to read the artist's name in the bottom left-hand corner. *Everly Kane.*

He walked slowly along the aisle. There were eight of them on display. All painted black and white with accents in various colors such as blue, or red, or orange. The art had a timeless, almost haunting aspect to it. Classy and clean.

He glanced at the prices. Only thirty-nine dollars for the prints. He picked up one from the shelf. It was about 20x20, smaller than the originals he'd seen. And he decided the paintings would look great in the movie theater. The originals, of course, not the prints.

He picked up another one of the prints as Everly arrived in the aisle.

"What are you doing?" she asked, smoothing some hair from her face.

"Checking out the local art," he said.

She set her hand on her hip. "Really?"

"I might buy a couple of prints."

She rolled her eyes. "Please, don't."

Austin walked toward her with the print in his hand. "How many have you done? Just these eight?"

"I have a few more," she said.

"I'd love to see them."

Everly's gaze held his. "You really don't have to do this, Austin. I mean it's nice of you to take an interest, but I know my talent level. Selling prints in a craft store is about as good as it gets."

He lifted his hand and moved a bit of her honey colored hair behind her ear.

She blinked, but she didn't pull away.

"I'm not doing it to be nice," he said, dropping his hand. "I'm doing it because I'm interested."

The edges of her mouth lifted. "Okay . . . You're kind of laying it on thick, you know."

"How's that working for you?" he asked.

"No bad, Mr. Architect, not bad."

He laughed.

She smiled, and he was pretty sure his heart grew a size. "So, wood glue?"

He looked down at his other hand. "Yep. And this print. Do you think you can ring me up?"

"Right this way, sir," she said with a smirk, then turned and walked toward the cash register.

Austin followed, wishing they could have lingered in the aisle a bit longer. But the store was busy, and Everly and Darla seemed to be the only two employees.

Darla was ringing up customers at the register, and Everly opened up the second register.

"I really should be giving you this print for free," Everly said, scanning the print, then the two bottles of wood glue.

"I'm sure it will be worth every penny." Okay, so he was being over the top. But it was kind of fun with Everly. Especially since it made her cheeks tinge pink.

"I'll give you the friends-of-employee discount," she said.

"Is there such a thing?" he asked.

She laughed. "Not exactly. So, you're just getting my discount."

"I'm fine paying the full price."

She gave him a pointed look, then typed something into the register. The price dropped by a few dollars.

Austin took out his wallet and ran his card through the older card reader. No chip reading at this shop. After he paid for his purchase, he said, "Well, I guess I'll see you soon, right?" There were now people waiting in line behind him, but he didn't care.

"Yep, tomorrow."

"Unless . . . you don't have dinner plans?"

Her eyes widened, and he wondered if he was pushing too hard. "We're open until nine tonight, and my dinner's going to be a turkey sandwich that I'll probably share with Snatches, thanks to you spoiling her rotten." She tilted her head, a smirk on those pretty lips of hers. "Thanks for the offer though."

She looked like she was about to say something else, but he could feel the gazes of the customers behind him. So, he walked out of the store with his wood glue, the art print, and a few more ideas forming in his mind.

Nine

"WHAT DO YOU MEAN YOU can't come?" Everly's mother asked over the phone. "Everyone is looking forward to seeing you."

Her mom was sweet to say so, although Everly knew it was a bit misguided. No one would miss her. Not at a brunch with Brock Hayes and his family.

"Is it Tom? Can he not come?"

Her mother already knew that Everly had cancelled Friday night because Tom couldn't make it. Well, Austin was right. It was now time to break up with Tom.

"No, he can't come, and actually we aren't seeing each other anymore," Everly said, making a mental note to text her sister the news as well.

It was so complicated keeping a lie straight.

"Oh no, what happened?" her mother asked.

After Austin had come into the craft store yesterday and shamelessly flirted with her, she realized that even going on a hike with Austin might put them in proximity to other town residents. Some of which might know her mother.

"Our schedules were forever conflicting," she said. "I feel like I never saw him." Everly closed her eyes. She was making a disaster out of this. "But today, I'm going on a hike with a new friend."

"Friend? Who's this friend, Everly? Are you doing those one-night stands I've heard about?"

Everly laughed. "No, Mom. I'm not . . . This guy's a friend."

"Oh, so it *is* a man," her mom said. "Who is he? What's his name? Is he from around here, or did you meet him at one of those craft fairs you go to?"

"His name is Austin, and he's doing the renovation on the movie theater in town," she said.

Her mom's questions only multiplied, and finally Everly said, "Mom, I've really got to go."

"But—"

"Love you, bye." Everly felt bad about cutting her mom off, but it was the only way she could stay sane. And she wanted to be sane on her date, or whatever it was, with Austin.

Six weeks—well, five weeks—and he'd be gone. So, they really would be friends.

Although Everly had seen what she hoped was interest in his eyes, they lived in different cities, had different lives, and probably different goals. Not that it mattered because going on a hike with him was just an activity. Show him around a bit. That was all.

Meow.

"I know, me too," Everly said, petting the cat's head. "Oh, is it really almost eleven?"

Everly scrambled off the loveseat. She was mostly ready, but she needed to double check her appearance, and . . . Her cell phone rang.

She cut her gaze to where she'd left it on the coffee table.

Austin's name flashed across the screen. Her stomach plummeted, and she wondered if he was cancelling. "Hello?" she asked in a breathless voice she hadn't been able to conceal.

"Hi."

"Hi." Her heart thundered as she waited for him to tell her he had to cancel. Of course. She shouldn't have been surprised. This was all too good to be true, right?

"Should I knock on the back door of the shop?" he said. "I mean, it's locked. Or are you coming down?"

"You're here?" she said, her voice a squeak. Dang it.

His voice was definitely amused when he replied, "We did agree on eleven, right?"

"Right." Breathless, again. "I'll be right down." She hung up. He was here. *He was here.* She hurried into her tiny bathroom and flipped on the light. She'd worn her hair in a messy bun. Maybe it should be in a ponytail instead so that it wouldn't potentially come out on the hike. She started over on her hair, using a bit of water to smooth it into a ponytail.

She was already feeling hot, so maybe she'd overdressed? Should she wear shorts instead of the capris she had on? Or maybe she should be wearing a darker t-shirt instead of the white one she had on. Were her earrings too long and dangly?

She wasn't sure how much time she took getting ready all over again, but by the time she walked out the back door of the craft shop, she was surprised that Austin was still waiting.

He was leaning against his truck, hands in his pockets. He wore khaki shorts and a light blue t-shirt that gave more definition to his chest and arms than she'd seen in his dress shirts. And yes, she was enjoying the view. His navy baseball cap was pulled low over his eyes, and he exuded a maleness that made her legs feel like water.

"Did you sleep in?" he asked before she could apologize.

"Um, I think I lost track of time," she said. "My mom

wouldn't take no for an answer over a text, and so she called. And then . . ." She stopped in front of him. There it was. His clean, showered scent. And this close, she could see the flecks of gold in his brown eyes.

"And then . . .?" he prompted, his mouth curving.

"I might have told her about you." She held her breath because she wasn't sure how Austin would react. They hadn't even been on a date technically, and he was leaving in a few weeks.

But he wasn't frowning or anything, so that was good, right?

"What did you tell her?" he asked in a low voice, his gaze trained on her.

"Your name and why you're in town," Everly said. "She peppered me with questions, but I said I had to go. And I did tell her that things with Tom and I were over."

He smiled then, and that smile did funny things to her belly.

"So, you're free and clear?" Austin asked, his smile still there.

"Yep."

"Then we'd better get going so we don't waste this beautiful day."

Would it be okay to kiss him yet? The wild thought sent a rush of heat through Everly. *Back off, woman,* she told herself as she walked with Austin around his truck. He opened the passenger door for her, and she had to pass by him to climb in. Yep. He smelled delicious.

She settled into her seat as he walked around to the driver's side. She could do this. Be casual. Have a nice day with a good-looking and definitely charming man. Keep him at a healthy distance while also doing a tiny bit of daydreaming.

As he pulled onto the street and headed out of town

toward the hills, Everly wondered how much he'd dated since his wife's passing. Did he keep things casual all of the time? Did he ever think about a more permanent relationship? Or would it be impossible for another woman to measure up to his wife?

"What's in the bag?" he asked as he slowed for a stoplight.

She looked down at the bag she'd brought, currently at her feet. "Oh, I brought a few snacks."

"A few?" the teasing in his voice made her smile.

"Maybe we'll want a granola bar on the drive back, or something."

He glanced over at her, amusement in his shaded eyes. She sort of wanted to take off his hat so she could get a better view of his chocolate brown eyes.

"When I first saw you with that bag, I was sure you were sneaking in food to the movie theater," he said. "But it seems that it goes everywhere with you."

She smirked. "It has all of my essentials in it."

"Essentials?" He chuckled. "Like what?"

"Well . . . my wallet and my phone for one."

He nodded. "Yeah, that makes sense, but that bag is the size of a small child."

"Whatever," she said. "I have a small bottle of lotion, Chapstick—well, a few choices in case I don't like the first choice."

Austin turned onto the road that led to the trailhead they'd decided to take. "What's your favorite Chapstick?"

Her eyebrows popped up. He was really into specifics. "Aloha Coconut. Want to try it?"

His eyes connected with hers briefly. "Maybe. What else is in there?"

"Water bottles. Pens. An art book. Sunglasses. My box of movie stubs."

They'd reached the parking lot. It was about half full. This hike was decent but not too crazy.

"Wait, an art book?" he asked, pulling into an empty parking space.

"Yeah, for notes or inspiration."

He shut off the truck and looked over at her. "Can I see it?"

She blinked in surprise. "Why?"

He leaned toward her, reaching for the bag on the floor. "Just curious."

Okay . . . maybe . . . Then she remembered a couple of her recent sketches. "No." She grabbed for the bag as Austin drew it toward him.

He didn't release his hold.

"I'm not ready to show anyone," she said. "They're doodles and completely amateur." She tugged harder, and he released the bag.

Pulling it against her chest, which she knew was a pretty immature thing to do, she said, "Sorry. You're only privy to the granola bars."

He didn't move back or seem put off. Instead, he smiled and lifted his hand. She held her breath as he plucked something out her hair.

"A leaf?" he said, holding up the small green leaf. His brow furrowed as if he couldn't figure out why she had a leaf in her hair.

The leaf was fake, and it must have fallen out of one of the artificial plants above the stairwell in the craft store.

She brushed the leaf off the palm of his hand, but before she could move back, he grasped her hand.

"I'd love to see your art book, Everly."

His fingers wrapped around hers was making her pulse skip beats. "Why?" she asked again, lamely.

He moved his thumb over her wrist. "To get to know you better."

The answer was simple, direct, and it had sent her pulse leaping ahead.

She would probably never, in a hundred years be able to figure out why she dug the art book out of her bag and handed it over, but that's what she did.

As Austin thumbed through the sketches, she held her breath. They were all of people. Some of them sketched when things were slow at the craft store, or other times she'd drawn from memory.

But instead of sketches of iconic movie stars, these were of ordinary people in Everly Falls.

"Who's this?" he asked, stopping on a picture of Brandy. "Your sister?"

"Yeah," she said.

Even sketched in pencil, Brandy was beautiful.

"You look like sisters," Austin murmured, turning the page to a second picture of Brandy.

"Well, she's the pretty sister, and I'm the creative sister." Although that wasn't exactly true. Brandy was plenty creative.

Austin paused and looked at her. "Your sister is pretty, but you're beautiful."

Her stomach flipped. "Wait until you see Brandy in person, you'll change your mind."

Austin's gaze hadn't left her face, and although his eyes were shadowed by the brim of his ballcap, that didn't decrease the intensity. "I won't change my mind," he said in a low voice.

Everly gave him a nervous smile. "I think we should go on our hike now."

"Almost done," he murmured, returning to the art book. He'd reached the middle. In a few pages, he'd find the ones of himself. She released a slow breath as he turned the page that showed him.

She'd sketched him sitting in the theater chair, his eyes closed.

Austin glanced up at her, his gaze questioning. "When did you draw this?"

She shrugged, even though she knew perfectly well she'd drawn it the same night she'd met him.

He turned the next page to a sketch of him at Marshall's coffee shop. He was sitting at a table with other people, although she hadn't defined their faces.

Before he could turn the next page, she pulled the notebook from his hands. "That's enough." Without looking at him, she tucked the book into her bag, then opened the truck door. She got out of the truck and shut the door. The warming air was fresh and gave her some breathing room from Austin.

He got out on his side, then walked around the truck. She shouldered her bag. "Ready?"

"Everly," Austin said, stopping close to her and bracing his hand on the truck next to her. "Do you have a hard time with compliments?"

She looked up at him, then away. "I'm fine with compliments, if that's what you're asking. But I don't really believe them."

Austin's fingers touched her chin, and he angled her face toward his. "Why not?"

He was still touching her, and his fingers were warm against her skin.

She released a breath and wrapped her hand tighter around her bag strap. "Maybe because I've failed at so many things, and it's not rocket science to see that others are more talented than me. Or prettier, like my sister. I mean, it never really bothered me. I love my sister. But when Brock . . . uh, dumped me for her, I suddenly became pro at insecurity."

Austin brushed his fingers across her jaw, then along her neck. When he rested his hand on her shoulder, she wanted to move closer. Press her face against his tanned neck. Breathe him in. Believe that he wasn't temporary in her town.

"Everly, you need to learn to take a compliment," he said. "Maybe we should practice."

"Oh really?"

"Really," he said moving closer.

Inches. That's how far apart they were.

"Everly, I think you look pretty today."

She refrained from rolling her eyes. "Okay . . ."

"*Thank you* is what you should say."

She scrunched her nose, then said, "Thank you."

He smiled. "That wasn't so hard, was it?" Then he lowered his voice. "You might want to sound a little more sincere next time."

"All right." Everly exhaled.

His hand slid over her shoulder and down her arm, creating a trail of goosebumps. "You smell great too."

Her gaze snapped to his. "That's overdoing it."

His eyes narrowed.

"Thank you," she said in an obedient tone. Then she reached up and snatched his hat. Plopping it on her head, she moved past him.

He lunged for her, but she dodged him, laughing.

Walking backwards, she continued toward the trailhead.

Austin shook his head, a smile on his face, then he locked the truck with his key fob. "Don't you have a hat or two in that bag of yours?"

"Nope." She continued walking up the trail, knowing he'd catch up easily enough. "Thank you for yours, though."

"I'll let you keep it on one condition."

She placed her hand on top of the ballcap as he drew closer. "What's that?"

"Let me see the rest of your sketches."

"I don't think so."

"Why not?" He was close enough to grab the hat if he wanted to now.

"Private."

"More sketches of me?" he teased.

"Maybe."

In a flash, he'd hauled her against him, and snatched the hat from her head. She twisted out of his grasp and grabbed for the hat. But his hands curled around her wrists and held her at arm's length.

"Fine," she said, her breathing shortened, her arms still locked by his hands. "You can have your dumb hat."

He chuckled and released his grip. But not all the way. He kept a hold of one of her wrists, then slid his fingers across her palm, interlocking their fingers.

Everly's heart about leapt out of her chest. What were the chances? The one man who she was pretty sure liked her, and who she was pretty sure she liked back, was only in town for a few weeks.

Ten

AUSTIN IGNORED THE MANTRA RUNNING through his mind: *Slow it down. You don't even know this woman.*

Except, that he did. Also, he wanted to know more.

But for now, he was content holding Everly's hand. She'd asked him about his daughter, so he told her more about Jessica and how she kept begging to come visit Everly Falls.

"You should bring her for a couple of days," she said, surprising him further.

"I think her attention would last about an hour, then she'd be bored," he said. "A job site only holds so much appeal."

"Any little girl loves to spend time with her dad," Everly said. "I think she'll surprise you."

Maybe she was right. "I'll think about it."

Everly cast him a smile, and as usual, it made something in his heart ping. She wore a pale pink lip gloss today, and he wondered if it was flavored. What was it about this woman that made him want to throw away his old precautions about dating? She also looked good in his ballcap. A few minutes after he had stolen it back, he set it on her head, and she'd been wearing it ever since.

"Hear that?" she asked, her hazel eyes focusing on him again.

"The sound of water?"

"Yep, we're getting close." She tugged at his hand as she increased her pace. "Come on."

He laughed. Maybe he could bring Jessica to this town for a day or two. Then she could meet Everly, and ... He didn't know.

They rounded the bend in the trail, and the landscape opened up to a wide pool and a waterfall dumping straight into it. A family was there ahead of them, and their two kids were in bathing suits and shorts. Another group of kids, teenagers, were horsing around and jumping off the falls into the deeper end of the pool.

Everly released Austin's hand and picked her way around the boulders, then sat on one of them and proceeded to take off her tennis shoes and socks.

So Austin did the same.

"Are we going in?"

"Just wading a little," she said. "Unless you want to jump off the waterfall."

He considered it for a second. "I don't think so."

Everly laughed. "That's what I thought."

"What do you mean?" He set his things by hers, then followed her into the water. The coolness was refreshing. The teen boys hooted as they each jumped off the waterfall.

Everly was already calf-deep when she turned to look at him. "You're kind of the preppy type, not really the daredevil type."

"And how would you know?"

She set her hands on her hips as he neared her. "Oh, I've

heard a bunch of your stories, Mr. Architect, and you were a pretty mellow kid. Basketball inside a gym, supervised summer camps, hours spent doodling at your desk."

"I've done some things . . ." he said. "Some dangerous things."

"Like what?" she challenged.

Austin pretended to think of his long, sordid past. "I can't think of anything right now. I must have blocked out all of my misdeeds." He was standing close enough to touch her now, but he didn't. He'd held her hand on the hike, and he hoped that she'd reciprocate.

"I don't believe you," she said with a grin.

He inched closer. "Well, you should."

"Oh yeah?" She was holding her ground, in fact, she seemed to have swayed toward him.

Another holler from one of the teen boys sounded, but Austin ignored it.

"Yeah," he said, keeping his gaze on hers.

"Come on then, daredevil," she said, reaching for his hand. "Show me your stuff."

His heart thumped as she threaded her warm fingers through hers.

"If I jump, you jump," he said.

She shrugged. "Okay."

And just like that, they headed toward the other side of the pool. She released his hand to climb up ahead of him. By the time they got to the top of the waterfall, the teen boys had hiked away.

"Where are they going?" Austin asked.

"There's another waterfall up the trail a ways."

Austin nodded and stepped to the place where the boys had been jumping off into the deepest part of the pool. The family that had been playing in the water was now packing up their things.

"Ready?" Everly's eyes gleamed as she joined him on the ledge. She pulled off his hat and handed it to him. Then she let out a whoop and jumped.

It all happened so quick that Austin could only stare. She landed with a splash, and he laughed as she bobbed to the surface.

"Come on in, it's warm in the deep end," she called.

Austin doubted that. But he tugged off his t-shirt then tossed the ballcap on top of it. He could fetch them later. No one else was in the pool now, and the family had already left. Everly swam several feet away to give him room to jump.

"Come on, *daredevil*," she hollered.

So he jumped.

The water wasn't warm at all. But when he came up to the surface, Everly was laughing, and that made it all worth it. He swam to her in a few strokes. Her hair was darker when wet, and her eyes seemed more green in the water than brown. "Do you take back what you said?"

"For calling you preppy?"

"Yeah."

"No." She moved away from him with a laugh, but he was faster.

Catching her around the waist, he hauled her against him. "Take it back," he rumbled next to her ear.

Her breathing had shortened, and so had his. Although the water was cold, he felt only warmth with her body against his.

"If you don't take it back," he said, "I'm going to dunk you."

She wriggled away from him with a laugh. He caught her around the waist and true to his word, dunked her. When she came up, she was gasping and laughing at the same time. He moved several feet away from her to avoid retaliation. Sure enough, she wiped the water from her face, then lunged.

Dodging her easily, he said, "I warned you."

She lunged again, and this time he let her catch him. When she pushed his shoulders down, he didn't budge.

"You're going to have to try harder than that," he teased.

So she placed both hands on top of his head and shoved him down. He still didn't go under, and he couldn't help but laugh.

"You're not being fair," she said, her arms now wrapped around his neck, bringing their bodies flush against each other.

Austin slid his hands around her back, keeping her close. "Life's not fair. Don't you already know that?"

Her face was only inches from his now, and he wondered if she knew how tempted he was to kiss her.

"I do know that." Her voice was softer now, barely audible above the sound of the waterfall. "But you're stronger and bigger than me, so you'll always have the physical advantage."

Her eyelashes were wet, and small lines of mascara trailed her cheek, but her lip gloss seemed unaffected by the water.

Everly wasn't pulling away, and he wasn't releasing his hold. So they swayed together with the water swirling from the power of the waterfall. Her arms about his neck warmed his skin where they touched his bare shoulders. The sunlight gleamed against her wet hair, making her look like she was some sort of ethereal water nymph.

He must have been staring at her without realizing it, because when she said his name, he felt like he was being dragged out of a dream state.

"Austin," she said, her fingers skimming the edge of his hair.

"Hmm?"

When she didn't answer, but continued to hold his gaze, he lowered his mouth to hers.

She tasted of cool water, warm sunshine, and laughter. Her fingers moved through his hair as she kissed him back. Her warm mouth on his sent all kinds of alarms through him, but he couldn't have pulled away if someone had dunked him. He'd just draw Everly down into the water with him since he had no plans of releasing her anytime soon.

Her kisses met his with the same urgency, same exploration, same curiosity. Sliding his hands lower, over her hips, she pressed even closer. And when she hummed against his mouth, he hoisted her legs around his waist as he deepened their kiss.

He'd never been so caught up in a kiss, so on fire with need, at least not in his recent memory. And perhaps never. He wasn't going to compare Everly to his wife, but he couldn't help it. Everly wasn't hiding her desire for him, and it only fueled him hotter. Rachel had always held back . . . at least with him . . .

"Austin," Everly whispered between the slow kisses that had replaced the hungry ones. "What are we doing?" Her body was trembling and her breathing rapid.

"Are you cold?" he asked, moving his kisses to her jaw, then to her neck.

"Hardly."

His laughter vibrated against her damp skin. "Good. Me neither."

She lifted her chin to give him better access. "We need to slow this down."

Austin pressed his mouth against the rapid pulse of her neck and breathed her in. "I know."

Her hands slid into his hair again, and the caress of her fingers sent a new rash of goosebumps across his skin. He moved his hands up her back, locking her against him. "Do you want my dry t-shirt?"

"I'm okay," she said. "I'll lay out on a boulder."

And Austin wouldn't mind watching her. He lifted his head and found her hazel eyes filled with questions. Ones he wasn't sure how to answer. "Okay." He kissed her lightly, once, twice. Then he kissed her harder because she was still wrapped around him, and he didn't want to let her go yet.

She kissed him back as her fingers found their way over his shoulders and down his biceps. Her touch trailed across his bare chest, sending darts of fire straight to his heart. He was out of breath now.

"Okay, you're right," he whispered against her mouth. Then slowly, reluctantly, he disentangled himself.

"Come on," he said, grasping her hand because he wanted to touch some part of her still. "Let's get you warm and dry."

She had goosebumps on her arms, and he kept his gaze mostly averted from how her wet clothing clung to the curves of her body. Once they reached the boulders where they'd left their shoes and her bag, he released her hand. "I'll grab my shirt and hat. Be back in a second."

She only smiled, then sat on the boulder and turned her face up toward the sun, closing her eyes.

He had to drag his gaze away from her and wade back through the water, then hike the short incline.

Returning, he handed over the shirt. "Here, change shirts, and we'll lay yours out to dry."

He turned around so he didn't see her change, but that didn't stop his imagination, which he needed to get firm control over again.

"Thanks, Austin," she said. "Your shirt fits great."

He chuckled and turned around. His shirt was definitely baggy on her, but that was probably a good thing right now. He took her wet shirt and laid it across a nearby boulder. Then he sat next to her where she'd laid back on the rock, her eyes closed.

There wasn't a lot of room, but he laid back too, his arm and body only inches from her.

The warm sun was intoxicating, and he kept his eyes closed, letting the rays dry his skin and hair. His shorts would take a lot longer, but he didn't mind. And he was pretty sure he could fall asleep right here and now, next to Everly, with a smile on his face.

"I still think you're preppy," she murmured.

He cracked an eye open to see that she was smiling. So, he leaned up on one elbow, then bent down and kissed her. She didn't move, just let him kiss her, slowly, and deliberately. He didn't need to touch her anywhere else for Austin to feel every other part of him burning up.

And he was pretty sure his heart wasn't far behind.

Eleven

KISSING AUSTIN WAS LIKE THE stuff of romance novels. Not only did he smell great, but he was an excellent kisser and definitely a gentleman. When things had gotten a little heated by the waterfall, he'd backed off. Which of course made her want to tell him not to, while all the same, she was grateful.

Because she needed to figure out what was going on. Between them.

As they drove back into town after their hike, Austin kept her hand in his. Holding his hand felt surprisingly comfortable, natural. Yes, she was freaking out inside a little—because Austin Hayes was a charming, generous, kind, and beautiful man, and she was liking him more and more by the hour—but she was trying to play it cool.

She'd had boyfriends before, most significantly Brock, so it wasn't like she was a recluse. But she hadn't let her heart open to anyone she'd dated since Brock. And she could feel it already cracking open now. Once they were out of the hills, her phone downloaded a bunch of texts, and they buzzed in rapid succession.

"Everything okay?" Austin asked, squeezing her hand.

She pulled her phone from her bag and glanced at her screen. Texts from her sister flashed—all with questions about Austin. Everly set her phone back in her bag. "Looks like my mom told Brandy that I was out with a guy who isn't Tom Middleston."

"Your sister knows Tom isn't real, right?"

"Right," she said. "And now she's wondering if *you're* real."

Austin slowed his truck at a light, then looked over at her, his brown eyes intense. "Do you want me to be real, Everly?"

Warmth bloomed in her chest, spreading to other parts of her body. The answer was a simple yes, but the outcome wasn't. Austin had a life outside of this town. A daughter who was waiting to see her daddy again.

Everly's life was here.

"I for one am glad you're real," she said, knowing that was probably the cheesiest line in all of history.

But Austin's mouth curved, and he leaned toward her. Then he kissed her. It was soft, yet lingering, and so . . . public.

A car honked behind them.

Austin straightened, and sure enough, the traffic light had turned green. She was gratified to see a blush creeping up his neck.

"I thought small town drivers were more patient," he said with a laugh.

Everly didn't speak for a moment. She couldn't. The simple, spontaneous kiss had left her wondering where all this was going. Because she was feeling things that went beyond a casual date.

"Hungry?" Austin asked, glancing over at her with a smile she was quickly becoming attached to.

"I look like a mess," she said. "That is, if you're thinking of going to one of the cafés or restaurants."

Austin's gaze raked over her as he slowed at a stop sign to make a turn. "You look great."

Everly scoffed. "It looks like we've been up to no good."

"I have no problem with that because it's true," he said with a grin.

She was positive she was bright red. "Sorry, but even though I told my mom and now my sister knows, I'm not ready for the interrogations."

He didn't seem bothered by her putting him off. "Take out, then? We can go eat at my place, or yours, or hit the park."

The park would still be too public, and since she hadn't been to Austin's, she said, "Let's go to your place."

He'd still have to take her home later, but that was okay too. Spending time with Austin had been an unexpected delight. And the kissing was . . . well, she had to figure that out because she wasn't about to set herself up for heartbreak. But as Austin pulled through a drive-thru, she wondered if it was already too late.

Once they had their orders, Austin drove to an older condo complex where he was renting a place for the duration of his stay. They packed the food inside, and Austin set it on the kitchen table.

The place wasn't much to speak of, and it made Everly curious about his place back home. Did he have a house? A condo? One he had shared with his wife and kid?

"I'm going to change," Austin said. "Do you want me to get you something to change into?"

Her shirt was dry, but her shorts still had a dampness to them. "Sure, if you have some sweats or something, that would be great."

"Be right back."

While he was gone, Everly sent a quick text to her sister.

Austin is real. And we're still on our date. I'll call you later tonight. She buried the phone back in her bag.

Everly moved to the fridge where a few drawings were taped to the door. They were obviously the handiwork of his daughter. Everly smiled at the childlike art of flowers and trees, and the bold script that read "I love you, Dad."

"This is sweet," she said when Austin came back into the room.

She looked over at him. He was wearing a dark brown shirt and well-worn jeans. His feet were bare. Austin looked good in everything he wore, she decided, and at the memory of what his bare torso looked like, she felt a flash of heat.

She swallowed and looked back at the drawings.

"Jessica loves to draw," Austin said, walking toward her and handing her a folded pair of sweats. But he didn't step away so that she could move past him to go change in the bathroom. Instead, he slid his arms around her waist from behind, and rested his chin on her shoulder.

"Is that how you got started with your art?" he asked. "As a little girl?"

She smiled as his breath feathered her exposed neck.

"Sort of," she said. "I was more into things like dirt and rocks. I used to play outside as much as possible. My mom bought me a paint set to try and keep me home more—keep me cleaner."

Austin chuckled, and his chest vibrated against her back. She relaxed into him. "I loved the way I could make paint into any shape I wanted to."

"Hmmm," he murmured.

Austin was making it hard to remember that she'd come over to his place to eat. "I'm going to go change," she said, moving out of his arms. "Where's the bathroom?"

"On the left side of the hall," he said, his gaze trailing over her. "Or you can use my bedroom on the right side. More room to change."

"Okay, thanks," she said. And that's how she ended up in his bedroom. It definitely looked like a temporary residence. Nothing on the walls. And he had two suitcases stacked in the corner. A single framed photo was on his nightstand, one of Austin, a woman, and a little girl who looked about three or four.

Everly couldn't stop herself from picking up the picture and examining it. She knew his wife's name was Rachel, and now that Everly was actually looking at a picture of her, it made her seem all the more real. The little girl was adorable, not surprising, and she took after Austin more than her mom. Jessica's eyes were brown, and her hair a medium brown. Her smile was impish, and she looked like the most content and loved little girl.

Rachel's dark hair was nearly black, and she looked like she'd been part of a magazine shoot. She was tall, willowy, and her eyes beautiful. She looked right into the camera as if she owned it, and while she leaned against Austin, she had an arm possessively about her little girl. As she should.

Because she was Jessica's mom.

Suddenly, Everly felt dowdy, and short, and pudgy. She'd been curvy since her early teens, and mostly she was good with it. But looking at Rachel, Everly wondered if she was even Austin's type.

Did this mean what was going on between them was only temporary? A fling?

Of course, it was. They both knew he was leaving in a few weeks. But that didn't make her feel better about anything.

Everly set the photo down, then quickly changed into the sweats. They bunched at her ankles, but at least they were completely dry, which was nice. She headed back into the kitchen where Austin had set out his food.

"Your phone's going nuts," he said as she sat down. He'd filled a couple of glasses with water.

Everly took a drink. "My sister is impatient, you know, and she wants details about this date."

Austin only smiled and unwrapped the sandwich he'd ordered. "What will you tell her?"

Everly didn't want to put a damper on the day spent with him, but seeing the picture of his wife had kind of already done that, at least for her. She looked down at the chicken salad she wasn't hungry for anymore. "I don't know, truthfully. I mean . . ." She raised her gaze to meet his. "I'm not sure what's happening between us. You're a great guy, Austin, really . . . great. But I live here. You're here for only a few weeks. And . . . I'm not really into flings, I guess. At least anymore. I mean, I'm twenty-seven, and well, I'm done playing games."

"Do you think I'm a player?" His brown eyes flashed dark, intense.

She felt like she'd swallowed a mouthful of sand, and she reached for her glass, not able to hold his gaze.

Austin placed his hand over her wrist, his fingers warm and gentle. "Everly. I'm not a player."

She gave a little nod.

"Everly, look at me."

She did, and what she saw in his eyes was what she wanted to believe was true. That he wasn't a player. That he liked her, and he wasn't looking for a fling either. That he was with her because he couldn't stay away from her. That they'd figure out things as they went.

"I'm not a player, okay?" he said again.

"Okay." It came out as a whisper.

"After Rachel died, things were hard," he said slowly. "I mean, everything was hard. My daughter had lost her mom. I'd lost my wife. It's impossible to explain the emptiness I felt. It felt never-ending. About six months after Rachel was gone, it seemed that some sort of alarm had gone off. Everyone thought it was okay to talk to me about dating again. About finding another woman. But no one knew the truth."

Everly couldn't move. She didn't know if she wanted to hear all of this personal stuff about Austin. They'd had a fun, carefree day together, but this . . . this was real life. He'd gone through a major tragedy.

"Before Rachel was diagnosed with cancer," he continued, "things between us were fragile."

Everly wasn't sure what he meant, and when he paused, as if considering what he might say next, only the ticking of the kitchen clock sounded between them.

"I knew things weren't perfect between us, but I hadn't realized how much our marriage had been derailed." Austin exhaled, then scrubbed a hand through his hair. "She'd been staying a few nights in the city—closer to her job at the salon— to save on commuting late at night. She kept late hours for her clients who worked fulltime jobs. I didn't like it, but I thought it made sense on one level."

Everly didn't move, didn't respond, just let him talk.

"About a month after her passing, I got an email from Taylor. I recognized the name of one of her coworkers. Expecting condolences, I opened the email. I quickly realized that the woman named Taylor was actually a man. Rachel had been living with him, and he wasn't gay."

Austin closed his eyes.

"What did you do?" Everly whispered.

"I called Taylor," Austin said. "I asked him point blank what the nature of his relationship had been with my wife." He paused as he rubbed his temples with both hands. His next words were etched with pain. "Taylor expressed condolences for my loss, but said he'd lost her too. He'd been in love with her, and he believed she'd been in love with him too. Taylor

91

said that Rachel had promised more than once to divorce me, but it clearly hadn't happened yet. Then the cancer came and ended everything."

Everly had no idea what to say, how to respond. The pain in his voice made her eyes burn with tears. He'd not only lost a wife, but had found out that he'd really lost her in every way possible.

"Austin," she said, her voice catching. "I'm so sorry. I can't even imagine what you went through."

He nodded, looking past her, as if he were remembering back. "When my mom and some of her friends started to talk to me about dating again, do you know what I thought?"

Everly shook her head.

"It was the last thing I wanted to do," he said. "To set myself up for another failure. To fall in love with a woman who had the power to betray me so horribly. I wanted nothing to do with dating. I only wanted to focus on my daughter. Jessica fulfilled everything I needed in life. I loved my career, and my daughter needed every bit of time that I could give her. I had nothing extra left to give, so I couldn't invest emotionally in another relationship. Plus, Jessica was still doing her own healing."

Everly's throat was thick. She drank some water, but it felt like she'd swallowed a rock.

Austin stared at the table top for a long moment, then he lifted his brown gaze to hers again. "From the moment I met you, or the moment you woke me up in the empty theater, I've been drawn to you, Everly."

She blinked. "You have?" she whispered.

"I can't explain it, but you fascinate me." His mouth curved. "You're so opposite of Rachel, so I thought maybe that was part of it. Maybe I was intrigued because you're so different."

She nodded, although her heart felt heavy. "That makes sense," she said in a small voice.

"But then I realized something else on our hike."

"What?" Could her heart pound any harder?

"I realized that you make me feel alive again." He brushed his fingers against her hand. "You make me feel like I've stepped into the light after sitting in a dark movie theater for months, possibly years."

Everly's eyes stung, and she blinked against the burning.

"I don't know what the future will bring," he said. "I'm only here for a short time, so I can't tell you what tomorrow will bring. But I'm not a player, Everly, and I really hope this isn't a fling."

It took approximately one point five seconds for Everly to pop out of her seat and throw her arms about his neck.

Austin laughed and tugged her onto his lap.

Then he kissed her. And she, of course, kissed him back.

"I'm so glad," she whispered after about a dozen kisses. "I didn't want you to be a fling either."

Twelve

"HI, SWEETIE," AUSTIN ANSWERED HIS phone.

"Hi, Daddy."

Jessica's voice sounded peppy, and that relieved Austin. Jessica calling him in the middle of the day was unusual, and he'd wondered if something was the matter.

"What's up?" he asked.

"I was sick, but now I'm better."

Austin walked away from the concessions at the movie theater where he'd been reviewing the plans with Jimmy. "Wait, what? You're sick?"

"I threw up," Jessica stated matter-of-factly. "So, Grandma picked me up early from camp. I don't know if I'll go tomorrow because I might be contagion."

"Contagious?"

"Yeah, that."

Austin paced the lobby. "How are you feeling now?"

"I'm bored."

Austin smiled at that, although he hated that his daughter

had been sick at camp. "I'm sure Grandma will keep you busy." His mother was the epitome of a busy body. If she wasn't cooking up a storm for the school bake sale, she was volunteering at the library, or running the girls scout group that Jessica was a part of.

"Grandma's craft fair is tomorrow, so she told me to watch the Disney Channel."

Austin grimaced. His mom was the organizer of the bi-annual craft fair, and he knew that would take up the entire weekend. No wonder she didn't have time to entertain her granddaughter. She'd been a nurse her entire career, and when she retired, she stayed busy in the community. Always volunteering for things. "What about Grandpa?"

"Grandma's making him do chores."

Austin chuckled at this. In his mind, he could hear his dad's good-natured grumble. "I'll bet. So, you're feeling better, but you can't go to camp tomorrow?"

Jessica sighed. "Yeah."

Austin glanced over at Jimmy, who was measuring everything for a second time before starting the official install. So far, things were on schedule, and Austin had planned on taking a half-day on Saturday to spend time with Everly. They had spent time together every night the past week, except for last night, and that was a long phone call. Tonight, they were going out to eat.

What if . . . "Hey, how about I pick you up, and you spend the weekend with me? I could take you back Sunday night. I know the drive is long, but—"

"Yes, Daddy, yes!"

Austin laughed. "Okay, let me talk to Grandma."

"Okay, Daddy," she said with a squeal.

His mother had literally been Jessica's saving grace, picking up the pieces when Austin had been numb with grief and despair. Moving them both forward in life. Becoming more than a grandmother, and going above and beyond what was expected. Austin had sold his home and found a condo closer to his parents. Jessica went to her grandparents after school most days until Austin was finished with work. As he waited for his mother to answer, he headed out of the theater into the bright, summer day. Jimmy didn't need to overhear every conversation with his family.

"Austin," his mother said, her tone harried. "Did Jessica tell you about being sick?"

"Yeah, Mom, that's what I wanted to talk to you about," he said, then explained his idea.

"Well, she'd certainly love that," his mom said, and he could hear Jessica celebrating in the background along with his dad's chuckle. "But are you sure? I know you're putting a rush on this job."

"I'm sure," he said. "We're on schedule, if not a little ahead." And he knew that he wanted Everly to meet Jessica, which meant that when he delivered his daughter back to his parents, she'd probably say something about the woman he was dating.

"I also need to tell you something," he said. "I've been dating a woman in Everly Falls."

His mother was silent for so long, that he wondered if they'd been disconnected.

"Mom, did you hear me?"

"I did." She exhaled. "What about Melissa?"

It was Austin's turn to exhale. Melissa Jensen was the daughter of one of his mother's closest friends. Divorced with two little kids, everyone thought they'd be the perfect match. Austin had met her at a neighborhood barbeque, and it only took about thirty seconds to know he wasn't interested in the woman. Her kids were completely wild, and she dressed like she was an eighteen-year-old pop star.

"Melissa and I aren't compatible," he said.

"You haven't given her a chance, Austin Hayes." His mother's tone was clipped.

Austin bristled, but he told himself to be patient. His mother's nerves were always on edge leading up to a craft fair event. Both he and his dad had learned not to argue with her during that time.

"Well, when I return home, and if I'm no longer seeing Everly, then I'll consider it." He'd said it only to appease his mom, but that seemed to make things worse.

"Everly? What kind of name is *that*? Isn't that the name of the *town*? Wait, is she one of those hicks who never washes her hair and cusses with relish? I know that Everly Falls is a small town, but really Austin, you can do better."

Austin blinked. What was going on with his mom? She was not a judgmental person, yet her words had been nasty. "Give me some credit, Mom. I'm only telling you about Everly because Jessica might bring her up. And yes, she's named after her town—ironic, I know—"

"You're going to bring Jessica into this?" His mother cut in. "Do you think that's wise, Austin? You know your daughter's feelings are still fragile. Maybe she should stay here . . . you know, until you're not dating that woman anymore."

Austin pinched the bridge of his nose. This was not anywhere close to the reaction he thought his mother might have. After two years, he was finally dating a woman, and without even seeing her or meeting her, his mom was suddenly possessive of Jessica.

Ironically, Everly's mom and sister had been begging to meet him. Which, ironically again, would take place on Sunday—when he'd now have Jessica with him. Austin took a slow, measured breath. "Mom, I'll be there in a couple hours to pick up Jessica. We can talk then, or later if you're too busy with the craft fair. But I need to wrap up a few things, then get on the road."

His mom went silent, and Austin watched a passing car. The driver waved, and although he had no idea who it was, Austin waved in return. It was how things were done in Everly Falls.

"All right, see you soon," she said. "I'll have lunch ready when you get here."

"I'll be fine," he said. "I can grab something on the way—" But his mother had already hung up.

Austin released a groan. Didn't he already have enough complications in his life? And now his mother was upset over a woman she'd never met. He pocketed his phone and rocked back on his heels as he watched the traffic pass in front of the theater. Well, traffic was a loose description, more like a handful of cars.

Maybe he should cancel his plans with Everly this weekend. Keep things exclusively daddy-daughter oriented. He'd love spending the one on one time with Jessica, yet . . . Things were complicated in his life, and for that very reason, it would be better if he introduced Everly to Jessica sooner than later. Then he would know . . . what exactly? . . . he wasn't sure. But he was sure he'd have more clarity on whatever this wild ride he and Everly were on.

It definitely wasn't a fling, but he couldn't ignore the giant clock ticking down the days and weeks until the theater was completed.

His mind made up, Austin turned from his view of the street and headed into the theater.

"Everything okay, boss?" Jimmy asked as Austin walked in.

"Yeah, but I've got to go pick up Jessica for the weekend."

Jimmy's bushy brows rose. "Now?"

"I'm afraid so," Austin said. "Can you be the boss for a few hours?"

The older man straightened. "Sure thing. Do I get the company credit card too?"

Austin chuckled. "Yep. Lunch is on me."

Jimmy grinned. He already had a company credit card, but the joke was a running thing between them.

A few minutes later, Austin was on his way out of town. The drive home was almost two hours, and he hoped his stop at his mom's would be short and not turn into an argument. He was about an hour into the drive when thoughts of Everly had begun to plague him. He should at least give her a head's up and the option of changing their plans. They both knew that dating in while he was away from his daughter wasn't exactly reality.

Oh, everything between them felt real, but work was only half of Austin's life.

What if... Everly wouldn't be a good fit for Jessica? What if Jessica seeing her dad with a woman he liked was hard on her? What if... Everly wasn't the woman he thought she was, or hoped she was?

He'd been burned before. Blindsided, really.

Austin checked the time. Everly was probably at work, but he couldn't text while driving, so he called her through the Bluetooth in the car. He could at least leave her a message, and then maybe she could text him what she wanted to do about this weekend.

But surprisingly, she answered, albeit a breathless hello.

"Oh, hey," he said, "Are you at work?"

"No, I'm leaving the bakery," she said. "My sister had a bit of a catering crisis, and I had to come help straighten it out. Apparently, the bakery isn't going to be able to get fresh blueberries in, so she's having to switch up her order to maybe raspberries."

"Raspberries for what?"

"For the cheesecake desserts."

Austin nodded even though Everly couldn't see him. "Did the raspberry pass your approval?"

He heard the smile in Everly's voice when she answered. "Most definitely." Then she released a sigh.

"Everything else okay?"

Everly seemed to hesitate before she answered. "Brandy and Brock both came which made me wonder why I had to be there too. I mean, two can decide as easily as three."

But Austin heard something else in her voice. "Is it awkward to be around Brock?"

"Oh, so awkward," she said with a nervous laugh. "And, he asked all about you. Like your parents' names and who your dad is descended from. All stuff I really couldn't answer."

"I'm sure we're related somehow, but it's distant."

"Yeah," she said. "But the weird thing was that Brock kept staring at me like he'd forgotten what I look like."

Austin frowned. "That is weird. Maybe he's realizing what he gave up."

"That's not funny," Everly said, her voice firmer than he'd heard it.

"I'm sorry," he said. "I didn't mean to imply—"

"I know," she said with a sigh. "I'm a little on edge, I guess. Walking back to the craft store will clear my head."

"From Brock?"

"From all things Brock," she said. "I can't believe I used to date him. Despite the staring, he's just pompous, you know. Like nothing is ever good enough, and everyone is wasting his time."

"Sorry."

"Oh, I'm not sorry," she said. "Which is a good thing to realize. I mean, you're the opposite."

"And that's a good thing, I hope?"

"Such a good thing." He liked hearing the smile back in her voice.

He was smiling too. "I'm glad, because I have a complication this weekend, and we might need to reschedule." He told her about Jessica's phone call, and how he was driving to pick her up now.

"Perfect," Everly said.

"You're glad I'm cancelling on you?"

"No." Everly laughed. "Perfect because Jessica can come with us."

This was what Austin had hoped to hear, but he didn't realize how relieved he felt until Everly suggested it. "Are you sure? I mean, it's totally okay if you want to have a kid-free weekend. You haven't ever met her, and—"

"Stop," Everly said. "I want to meet your daughter, so if you're okay with that, I'm in."

"I'm definitely okay with it . . ." he said in a slow voice, his pulse gathering speed. "If you're okay with it."

"I'm honored, truly," Everly said in a soft voice.

If he was with her in person, he would have grabbed her and kissed her. As it was, he had a permanent grin. "Then I'll call you when we get back in town, and we'll go from there."

He loved the lightness of her tone when she said, "Sounds great, Austin. Can't wait to meet your daughter."

Nothing could dampen Austin's good mood. Not even his mother's wary gaze when she opened the front door of her house. Or his dad's furrowed brows, which only indicated he'd received an earful from Mom about the woman Austin was dating.

Jessica had no such reservations, and he pulled her into a

bear hug, then drew away to gaze into her brown eyes—so much like his. "You've grown an inch, sweetie."

"No, I haven't," she said with a giggle. "Look, Grandma braided my hair."

Jessica's brown hair was known for its unruliness. *How long will it stay in the braid?* he wondered. *Hopefully three days.*

He ate a quick lunch with Jessica and his parents, mostly because his mom had fixed egg salad sandwiches, even though Austin wasn't hungry. But it was hard to turn down his mom's homemade food. Thankfully, Jessica was permitted to nibble since she was still recovering, and Austin didn't have to wait through the long minutes of his mother cajoling Jessica to eat more.

Once lunch was cleared, his mom gave Jessica a hug, then released her only to set her hands on her hips while she met Austin's gaze. "Take things easy with her, all right? She's better but had a rough morning."

"I will, don't worry," Austin said as smoothly as he could. Then he grasped Jessica's hand, and picked up her pink Barbie decal suitcase with his other hand.

Jessica skipped alongside him, apparently full of energy as they walked to his truck. He settled her onto the back seat, then leaned over and kissed her forehead. "Ready?"

She grinned. "Ready!"

"That's my girl."

He climbed into the driver's side, then waved to both of his parents who were watching from the front porch, trepidation in both of their gazes.

"I love you, Daddy," Jessica said.

The tension that had been building inside Austin for the past twenty minutes immediately eased. He glanced in the rearview mirror to see his beautiful daughter searching through her pink backpack, which matched her suitcase. She was coming to Everly Falls with him, and he was more than excited about it. Nothing else mattered right now. "I love you, too, sweetie."

Thirteen

EVERLY SHOULD HAVE KNOWN THE moment her mother walked into the craft store that trouble was brewing. Lydia Kane never did anything without a purpose, and Everly doubted her mom was in need of craft supplies since Brandy's wedding was being completely planned by a wedding company.

Their mother looked more like Brandy, with pale blonde hair and effortless grace. Her heels clicked on the floor as she neared Everly where she was putting up sale prices on their needlepoint aisle. It had been a couple hours since she'd talked to Austin, and she assumed he was halfway back by now. She'd enjoyed the afternoon of basking in their most recent conversation, the one in which he said he wanted her to meet his daughter.

Everly had truly been honored, and flattered, and she was buzzing with anticipation.

Until now. Her mother's pinched brows could deflate anyone's good day.

"Hi, Mom," Everly said, grateful the store wasn't

crowded, and that her boss was deep in conversation with Mrs. Allred about one thing or another.

Her mother stopped, set her hands on her hips, and said, "Brandy said you're upset. What's wrong? Is it that new man you're dating? The out-of-towner with a kid? You know you're walking straight into complicated with that one."

Before her mom could disparage everything about Austin's very existence, Everly cut in. "I'm not upset. I hope you didn't come all the way over here to question me, because I don't know what Brandy is talking about."

Everly was going to kill Brandy. They both knew how their mom could blow things out of proportion in about two seconds flat.

"Then what happened at the bakery?" her mom said, not letting this go. "Brandy said you acted like you didn't care if they chose raspberry, cherry, or strawberries. You even said that plain chocolate sounded good."

At this, Everly set down the sale signs on the nearest shelf and turned to face her mom fully. On one hand, she supposed that every mother and daughter pair went a little crazy when getting ready for a wedding, but they needed to leave her out of it. Especially considering who Brandy was marrying.

"They all sound good," Everly said in a dry tone. "It's cheesecake. What can go wrong?"

Her mother's eyes narrowed. "Are you still mad at Brandy for stealing Brock?"

Everly sputtered. "No, Mom. Oh my gosh. How can you say that?"

"Because." Her mother inched closer, lowering her already hushed voice. "You're dating men left and right. Each week you're with a different man, and I don't want my daughter to be the town floozy."

At this, Everly squeezed her eyes shut and gritted her teeth. She didn't know whether to cry or laugh.

"Honey, it's not too late," her mother said, touching her arm. "Get off those dreadful dating apps. Meet men the normal way. They're out there, I promise."

Everly opened her eyes to gaze into her mother's blue eyes—much like Brandy's. "Mom, I made up Tom Middleston so that you'd stop harping on my about my love life."

Her mother's mouth formed an O. "W-what?"

"That's right," Everly said, her pulse skyrocketing. "Tom wasn't real."

"He's not a lawyer who was just too busy?"

"Nope."

"Oh, goodness," her mother said, bringing a hand to her mouth. "I was afraid this would happen."

"What?"

"I don't think you've dealt with your breakup with Brock properly. I think you need to see a therapist."

If a hole opened right in front of her on the store floor, Everly wouldn't have been surprised. And then she would have climbed right into it.

"Have you been fantasizing about Austin, then? I did ask Mayor Sanders about him, and she did confirm he was hired for the renovation."

"You asked the mayor about Austin Hayes?"

Her mother lifted her chin. "I certainly did. At least Austin's real, but honey, you really should see someone."

"Austin is real, and we really are dating." The doubt and concern didn't leave her mother's eyes though. Everly took out her phone and pulled up the call log, showing her mom the most recent call from Austin. Then she showed her the string of texts.

Despite all of that, her mom didn't relax. "What about his child? Did you know his wife died of cancer? The mayor told me—"

106

"Mom," Everly said. "Of course I know about Austin's daughter, Jessica, and his wife, Rachel. We're dating. I'm not making that up, and I don't need a therapist. At least I didn't until you walked in here."

"Everly Jane Kane," her mother spat out. "You are out of line."

Everly simply stared at her mother, hoping the woman would see the irony of her statement.

"Everly?" her boss, Darla, called. "Can you cover the register?"

"Happy to," Everly called back. She glanced toward the register to see an older couple waiting. She looked at her mother once again. "I'm sorry for making up Tom Middleston, but if you can't get over your determination to throw me into therapy because you think I'm pining over Brock Hayes, then I'm not going to be coming to the Sunday brunch."

Her mother's eyes rounded.

"I'm going to say this one final time," Everly continued. "I'm not brokenhearted over Brock. I'm happy for Brandy. Now, can we all move on with our lives?"

Everly strode away, because her voice had cracked on the last word, and the last thing she needed to do was fight back tears as she rang up the customers buying Fourth of July decorations.

She helped the customers, and a few other people who'd apparently been in the store. Once the mini-rush cleared up, her mom had left, and Everly felt a hole of guilt growing inside her.

But she'd only spoken the truth, and now the weight of her made-up Tom Middleston was gone. On her next break, she checked her phone, and sure enough, Brandy had sent several texts, all at different times.

Mom told me you're mad at her.

Sorry if I stirred things up.

I just don't want you to be upset about all of this.

Brock was also concerned, so it wasn't just me.

I'm glad you told Mom that Tom was fake.

Please come to the brunch on Sunday.

You should bring Austin! We all want to meet him.

What followed was a series of heart emojis.

Everly replied with a single line: *I'll keep you posted.*

For now, she needed a break. From her mom and sister, from the wedding plans, from Brock's part in everything.

She needed Austin.

Where was he now? At the theater with his daughter? Eating someplace? At his apartment? Maybe he'd taken her to the park? Maybe he'd come by the shop?

Every time the shop door opened, Everly's gaze snapped to whoever entered. Austin didn't show, and she checked her phone more than she should. No calls or texts from him. By the time her shift ended at seven, Everly knew Austin should have been back in town several hours ago. What if he hadn't come back but had decided to spend the weekend at home?

For some reason, this sent her pulse jumping. Having him so far away made her feel like the past week might have been a dream. Or some crazy, heady fluke.

"I'm heading out now, Darla," Everly said as she straightened a final display of candles.

"All right, dear," Darla said. "Say hi to that man of yours."

Everly smiled, although she didn't feel like smiling. She was too anxious, too worried, and too many insecurities were plaguing her. She walked to the back of the craft store and opened the door leading up to the stairs.

She trudged up the stairs and scooped Snatches into her arms. The cat started to purr, her little body rumbling. Everly sat on her loveseat, closed her eyes and cradled the furry creature. She tried to empty her mind of all worries, to forget her argument with her mom, her sister's oozing concern, and the fact that Austin hadn't called.

When her phone did ring, Everly snapped her eyes open. She'd almost dozed off, and so it took her a minute to orient herself and see that Austin was calling. Her heart slammed into her throat, and she answered with a breathless, "Hello?"

Would he tell her that he'd stayed in his hometown, or that he'd be hanging out with his daughter exclusively this weekend?

"Hi," he said. "You hungry?"

Relief swept through her like an August forest fire. "Starving," she said. Had her voice squeaked?

Austin chuckled, and her eyes burned with tears of relief. She was being ridiculous, but Austin had called her, he was still here, he was still in her life.

"What sounds good?" he asked, his deep voice rumbling through the phone. A voice she loved.

"How about you decide, or better yet, your daughter," Everly said. "Is she with you?"

"Yep, Jessica's here," he said, his tone warm. "Do you seriously want me to ask her? You might regret it."

"Ask her," Everly said. "I'm not picky."

"Okay," Austin said.

Everly kissed the top of Snatches head, then she heard Austin's deep voice speaking to Jessica, followed by her higher pitched reply.

Everly couldn't make out their conversation, but then Austin came back on the line. "She wants pizza."

Everly smiled. "Sounds good to me."

"Are you sure?" he asked, and the words felt weighted. He wasn't just asking her if she liked pizza, but if she would spend her time with him and his daughter.

Everly would have shouted her answer, but that might have confirmed her mother's suggestion for a therapist, so instead, she said, "I'm sure. What time?"

"Um, fifteen minutes?" he asked. "She'll get grumpy if I don't feed her soon. She's already gone through all the snacks she brought with her."

"No problem. Should I meet you somewhere, or . . ."

"We'll head over."

"Okay." When Everly hung up, she squeezed Snatches a bit too tightly, then jumped to her feet and hurried to her tiny closet.

After three clothing changes, and trying to repair her hair and makeup, she hurried down the stairs. She'd settled on one of her newer sundresses that was blue with tiny polka dots. The store was still open, so she slipped out the back door, not wanting any customers to spot her and think she was on shift.

She heard the sound of Austin's truck before she saw it, and her heart was already thumping when she caught sight of it pulling into the parking lot.

She headed toward the truck as Austin stopped. He climbed out, surprising her since she thought she would just hop in. And wow, was he a sight for sore eyes. Gone was anything resembling a dress shirt. He wore jeans and an older t-shirt that did nothing to conceal his broad shoulders and defined chest.

Austin walked toward her, and knowing his daughter was in his car, she didn't know how to greet him. Apparently, he wasn't worried about that detail.

He pulled her into a hug, a surprisingly tight one, and she held on.

"I missed you," he whispered against her ear.

"I missed you too," she said, her throat feeling tight.

His hands moved slowly up her back, and that's when she heard someone say, "Daddy!"

Austin released a breath, then drew away, and his gaze locked on Everly. "Are you sure you're okay with this?"

Everly grasped his hand and squeezed. "Yes, now stop asking."

He flashed her a smile, then keeping her hand in his, he led her to the passenger side where he opened the back door to the cab of the truck.

Jessica Hayes was a mini-me of her father, albeit the feminine little girl version.

"Hi, I'm Everly, what's your name?"

"Jessica!" she said.

Everly smiled. "Great to meet you." She held out her hand, and Jessica promptly shook it.

"I love your backpack," Everly said, spying the pink, sparkly bag next to Jessica. "Who's your favorite barbie?"

Jessica's eyes widened, and so did her smile. "Rapunzel," she said. "Do you want to see?"

"Sure," Everly said and watched as Jessica dug into her bag, then produced a doll.

"Oh, she's great," Everly said, taking a hold of the doll and examining her purple gown. "I love her shoes too. What happened to her earrings?"

Jessica's expression fell. "They keep falling out."

Everly lifted her own bag. "I work at a craft store, and we have all kinds of things there. One of my favorite things is the barbie glue."

"Barbie's have their own glue?"

"Sure do." Everly located the small tube of craft glue. "When you find the earrings, let me know, and we can glue them on."

"Okay," Jessica said, a pleased smile on her face. She started to dig through her backpack.

"Thank you," Austin whispered against her ear,

wrapping his arm about her waist. "And I can't believe you have glue in your bag."

She turned her head to see his grin. He was only inches from her. So tempting to kiss him, yet she didn't know the rules around his daughter. So, she edged around him and moved to the passenger door.

Austin opened the door for her, and she climbed in, her stomach in knots of excitement. So far, so good. Jessica was like any other little girl. Everly could do this.

Austin settled into the driver's seat, then winked at her, and put the truck into drive.

Had she ever blushed at a wink? Well, she had now.

Fourteen

AUSTIN HAD NEVER HEARD JESSICA chatter so much, and he marveled at the intricacies of the Barbie world. Everly seemed to have no problem keeping up, and she even asked questions that only sent Jessica on another excited tangent.

All through their pizza dinner, and then during their walk to the park, Jessica talked. She even held Everly's hand. Jessica walked between the two adults, holding each of their hands. When she finally broke off, after Everly encouraged her to try out the jungle gym in the light of the setting sun, Austin could only stare after her in wonder.

A few other kids were there with their families, and Jessica joined in, easily playing with them.

Everly moved to his side, he grasped her hand and linked their fingers together.

"Wow," he said. "I had no idea she had all of that in her. It's like Barbies are an entire universe."

Everly laughed. "She's adorable."

Austin looked down at Everly and saw that she was sincere. "You're not . . . um, put off by all of this?"

Her forehead creased. "By Jessica? No, why would I be?"

He turned more fully to her. Her hair was golden in the glow of the sunset, and he'd been appreciating her strappy blue dress all evening. "Because dating me is not just about dating me . . . Jessica is part of the package too."

Her lips curved. "It's a great package though, with an amazing guy and a sweet little girl."

Austin wanted to lean down and kiss Everly right now, but they were in a very public place. And he figured that easing Jessica into things was the best idea. He didn't have to wonder what she thought of Everly—it was obvious his daughter was smitten.

"Watch this!" Jessica's voice interrupted Austin's internal battle of whether to kiss Everly right now.

Everly turned her gaze, and Austin looked over in time to see Jessica jump out of a swing and land on the ground.

Everly released his hand and clapped. "Great job!"

"Um, is that safe?"

"It's fine." She slipped an arm about his waist. "You're a great dad, Austin."

He draped his arm about her shoulders and pulled her close. Breathing in her scent of flowers and sunshine, with the warm summer breeze floating around them, he wondered if he'd ever had a more perfect night.

Jessica teamed up with another young girl, and they started playing a game of tag of which the rules were a mystery to him. "She makes friends so easily," he said. "I mean, at my mom's, there aren't any kids in the neighborhood since it's mostly retired folks. That's why going to the summer camp is great for social interaction."

"What about during the school year?" Everly asked. "She probably has plenty of friends there."

"Yeah, but she goes to my mom's after school until I'm

finished with work," he said. "Playdates are impossible since I work a lot of Saturdays as well."

Everly nodded, her head moving against his shoulder. "Smaller communities like ours are great for neighborhood friends. You know, quiet streets, lemonade stands in the summer, friendly neighbors. Maybe you should move here. It's a great place to raise a kid."

Austin stilled. He knew it was an off-hand comment, but she'd hit a sore point. He'd never thought he'd be living the apartment life as a single dad. And his daughter was growing up differently than he'd ever expected. Outside of school, Jessica was around adults all of the time unless he paid for her to go to a summer camp.

He traced his fingers over her shoulder. "I do like a few things about *Everly* Falls."

He heard the smile in Everly's voice when she said, "Oh, like what things?"

"Let's see . . . there's a charming theater, and Marshall's Coffee Shop has pretty good coffee."

Everly tightened her hold on his waist.

"The pizza isn't bad, and there's this great craft store that sells wood glue that's top notch."

Everly laughed. "And you get a discount."

"Yep." He smiled down at her. Her hazel eyes were nearly brown in the approaching twilight. "But there's one thing that's my favorite."

She tilted her head. "What's that, Mr. Architect?"

"You," he whispered.

Her cheeks flushed a pretty pink, her eyes sparkling. If they weren't in a public park and his daughter wasn't a half-dozen yards away, he would have kissed her senseless.

As it was, his pulse hummed, and his skin buzzed at her nearness.

"You know what would make this town the most perfect place in the world to live?" she whispered.

He lowered his head, closer to her, so that he could breathe her in. "What?"

"You." Everly tapped his chest. "And Jessica."

The pink on her cheeks had darkened, and he was pretty sure her heart was hammering as much as his. And he no longer cared that they were in public. Austin lifted his hand and ran his thumb across her jaw, then moved his thumb to her soft lips. She exhaled a warm breath against his fingers. Before he could kiss her, Jessica called, "Daddy! Everly! Watch us!"

He hid a groan and looked over at the playground. Jessica and her new friend were on the teeter totter, but they were both standing and bending over to hold on.

"I don't think that's safe," he called out. He released Everly and strode over at the same moment another parent headed toward Jessica's friend.

"Lizzy," the other man said. "That's not safe. Why don't you get on the swings, and I'll push you."

"Okay," Lizzy said, a girl with curly blonde hair. "Can you push Jessica too?"

The man glanced at Austin, and Austin said, "I'll push Jessica."

"I'm Brad," the other father said.

"Austin."

They shook hands, and a moment later they were both standing next to each other, pushing their daughters on the swings.

"You're new in town, right?" Brad asked.

"Yeah, I'm overseeing the theater renovation," he said. "I brought my daughter here for the weekend."

Brad's gaze cut to Everly, who had started talking to a

woman on the other side of the playground. "Oh, you must be the Austin who Everly is dating."

Austin tried not to look stunned. "Yes, that's right."

Brad chuckled. "Sorry for the intrusion. My mother is the hair stylist for Everly's mother." He shrugged. "Small town talk, I guess."

"Everly warned me." Surprisingly, Austin wasn't annoyed. "How old is your daughter?"

"She'll be eight next week," Brad said, smoothly transitioning. "Love this age. We have a couple of older kids, and they'd rather hang out with their friends than go to the park with their parents, know what I mean?"

"Jessica's my only child," Austin said. "But I'm pretty sure her excitement to be with Daddy won't be happening when she's a teen."

"So true," Brad said with a laugh. "Hey, if you have Jessica in town next weekend, I'm sure Lizzy would love to have her over for her birthday party. Her birthday's on the Fourth of July, but we always do something just for her the night before."

"Can she come? Daddy, please?" Lizzy called from her swing.

"Oops," Brad said. "Probably should have spoken a little quieter."

"Can I go, Dad?" Jessica called out.

Austin looked between the girls. "How about I talk to Grandma and see what's going on back home, then we'll decide."

"Yay!" Jessica shouted.

The two girls were thick as thieves over the next thirty minutes as the sky darkened to a deep purple. The lights in the park switched on, and teenagers started to populate the nearby skate park with their bikes and skate boards. At the same time a group of girls began a pickup game of sand volleyball.

"This park really comes alive at night," Austin commented as he stood on the side of the playground with Brad.

"Yeah, summer's like that here," he said. "Once the day cools off, everyone gets their second wind."

Austin chatted with Brad for a few more minutes, then Everly and the woman walked over. Turned out that the woman was Brad's wife, Marci, her blonde hair almost identical to Lizzy's. The conversation between the four of them was friendly, but Austin didn't mistake the curiosity in Marci's gaze as she glanced from him to Everly.

After everyone said good night, Jessica made it her sole mission to beg to return next weekend for Lizzy's birthday party.

"Did you get her dad's cell phone number?" Jessica said, never one to miss a thing.

"I did," Austin said, "And like I told you, I need to talk to Grandma."

"Then call her right now!"

Austin exhaled. "We'll talk to her when I drop you off on Sunday, okay? Now we need to get you to bed because we have a big day tomorrow."

This seemed to mollify Jessica for about two minutes. Once they were in the truck, she started to beg again. "Call Grandma. It's not *her* bedtime, and I don't want to miss the party."

Austin fired up the truck and tried to keep the impatience out of his voice. "Grandma is very busy with the craft fair this weekend, remember? Plus, next weekend is the Fourth of July, and Grandma might be sad if you were gone."

"All right," Jessica said, a pout in her voice. "But call her as soon as I wake up in the morning."

"Hey, Jessica," Everly said, "I wanted to ask if you know how to make bracelets?"

Austin glanced over at Everly. He wasn't sure where she was going with this, but it had effectively changed the conversation because Jessica said in a much more cheerful tone, "What kind of bracelets?"

"Ones with sparkly pink and purple beads," Everly said. "We have a brand-new bracelet kit in my store, and I really want to try it out. But I need someone to help me. Will you help me?"

"Okay," Jessica said. "Can I make one for my grandma?"

"Sure," Everly said in easy tone. "We can make as many as you'd like. Maybe we can even give one to Lizzy."

"Do you know where she lives?" Jessica's tone sounded incredulous.

"I do," Everly said, laughter in her tone.

They were near the craft shop, and Austin parked next to the back door.

"See you tomorrow, Jessica," Everly said. "Remember, go to bed nicely for your dad like a big girl. I really need a big girl's help tomorrow."

"Okay!"

Austin held back a chuckle as he climbed out of the truck. He wasn't sure about the staying power of Jessica's agreement, but he was impressed that Everly had tried. She waited for him to come around the front of the truck and open her door. Then she slid out, and he clasped her hand as he walked with her to the back door of the shop

"Thanks for that," he said. "She can be pretty headstrong."

"Headstrong doesn't bother me," Everly said, casting a smile up at him.

He waited while Everly unlocked the door, and before she

could pull it open, he said, "If you want to back out of our plans tomorrow, I understand."

Everly turned and looked up at him. "I'm not backing out unless you want me to."

He held her gaze. There was so much he wanted to say, not to mention that he wanted to kiss her. "I don't want you to back out."

"Good." She pulled open the door and stepped through the doorway. Then she grasped his shirt and drew him toward her so that the door blocked Jessica's view of them for a moment.

Everly lifted up on her toes and pressed her mouth against his. The kiss was much too short, but very sweet, and only made him wish he didn't have to say goodbye to her tonight. He kept his hands on the doorframe because he knew if he touched her more than kissing her, it would be even harder to let her go.

But he had a kid in the truck, and he didn't want to get her too far off her routine. "Thank you for everything," he whispered against Everly's mouth. "You're an angel."

She smiled, then twined her arms about his neck and kissed him once more. "See you tomorrow."

He really wanted to stay in her space, keep her close. Instead, he drew back and waited until she shut and locked the door. Then he strode back to his truck.

"What took you so long?" Jessica asked as he settled into his seat.

"I had to say goodbye to Everly," he said, glancing back at her. She was finally looking sleepy, and hopefully, that meant she'd go to bet without any fuss.

As if on cue, Jessica yawned. "I wish it was tomorrow."

"Why's that?" Austin asked with a chuckle.

"Then I can make bracelets with Everly."

"I wish it was tomorrow, too," Austin said.

Fifteen

EVERLY OPENED HER EYES TO see a pair of light blue eyes staring back at her.

Meow.

"Hi, kitty," Everly said. "Are you hungry?"

Meow.

"All right, hang on." She burrowed deeper into her covers, while sticking one hand out to pet Scratches. Everly was content to wake up slowly. It was Sunday morning, and today would be another day with Austin and Jessica.

Spending most of the day yesterday with Austin and Jessica had been more fun than she could have imagined. Austin had even helped them make bracelets. They made over a dozen since Jessica declared she wanted to make them for her camp friends.

Then they'd gone on the same hike where Everly and Austin had first kissed. This time they didn't jump off the waterfall or find any privacy to revisit their first kiss, but it was fun to watch Jessica splash in the water. She also made two new friends, Damon and Penny. Everly knew both of the kids' families, and she was starting to get used to the knowing looks from the town residents.

Today . . . today, Austin and Jessica were coming to the brunch with her family. At this thought, the butterflies awakened in her stomach. She'd already warned Brandy to be mellow, but there was nothing Everly could do about her mom. Her mom would likely ask a million questions, and who knew how she'd react to Jessica?

Despite this worry, Everly smiled. Austin had made no secret about his interest in her, and had no problem holding her hand in public, and truthfully, Everly felt flattered about that. And she sort of couldn't wait to see Brock's reaction when he met Austin, who was of course, superior to Brock in every way.

Austin was more of a gentleman, more generous, and made her feel like she was the only woman he was interested in. . . . Of course, the tiniest niggling thought kept trying to surface. What would happen when Austin met Brandy? The beautiful, flawless Kane sister?

Perhaps Everly had gotten completely over Brock, but she'd never get over the fact that it was her very own sister who had come between them.

Meow.

"You're right," Everly murmured to her cat. "I need to have more faith in Austin, and more faith in what's happening between us." With everyone they'd encountered yesterday, Austin had been friendly and open. He'd even asked questions about what they liked about living in Everly Falls. She couldn't deny that she'd felt tingly all over when he talked like that— when he acted like he might consider moving here.

Although it might not matter because Everly was pretty sure that if things kept moving forward between them, she'd be willing to relocate.

"What do you think about moving, Snatches?" she said, pulling the purring cat close. "A new town? A new life?"

Meow.

"That's what I think, too," Everly said with a laugh. Then she released the cat and climbed out of bed. After feeding Snatches, she cracked open the window—the cat's favorite mode of escape.

Everly showered and dressed, her heart light and hopeful. Showing up to the family brunch with Austin would be so much better than showing up alone like she usually did. Less than an hour later, Austin's truck pulled up alongside the curb in front of the store. She'd told him to meet her there since he'd texted he was running late. Saving even a few minutes would make a difference to her mom, who'd already called twice. Once to make sure she was still coming, and a second time to ask where she was.

"I'm on my way," Everly said into the phone. "Austin is running late. Life is more complicated with a child."

"You don't have to tell me that," her mom snapped.

And the day had suddenly dimmed. Her mom was already on edge, and Everly would soon follow if she didn't pull herself out of it right now. "I didn't mean it that way, Mom. Look, I see his truck. We'll be there as soon as possible. You can start without us, it's seriously okay."

"We're going to wait, but you know how important it is to me to start a meal on time. Does Austin always run late?"

Why did her mom's tone sound judgy? Her mom had been pushing her for months to start dating, and now that she was . . . Maybe Everly was being hypersensitive herself. She decided not to answer her mom's question. "See you in a few minutes."

She hung up without allowing her mom to respond. Then she walked toward the curb as Austin's white truck slowed.

She reached for the door handle when it stopped, tugging it open.

"Hey, guys," Everly said, smiling at Jessica then at Austin. The little girl looked like she'd been crying, and Austin's face was grim.

"Are you okay, honey?" Everly asked Jessica as she climbed into the truck. She didn't know where *honey* popped up, but it had.

"Can you do my hair?" Jessica asked, her voice trembling. "Daddy doesn't know how."

"I know how," Austin said with a sigh that barely concealed his frustration.

It didn't take Everly long to assess the situation, especially after seeing the disarray of Jessica's hair. "I can help," Everly said, opening the door again.

"What are you doing?" Austin asked, his tone faintly alarmed.

"I'm going to sit by Jessica while you drive," she said. "I can do her hair on the way."

When she settled next to Jessica, Austin pulled away from the curb.

Everly held back a smile as she examined the little girl's hair. The ponytail was crooked, and the hair that should have been smoothed was bumpy. This was a crisis she could help with.

"Do you have a hair brush?" Everly asked.

Jessica's eyes filled with tears. "Daddy only has a comb."

"It's okay, honey," she said, "I have one in my bag." She snatched her bag from the front seat, then dug through. In seconds, she had the hair brush. Next, she gently pulled out the ponytail holder that was the kind of elastic found on rolled up newspapers.

"Ouch," Jessica complained.

"Sorry," Everly murmured.

Austin's jaw had tightened.

"I have a ponytail holder that won't hurt," Everly said, digging through her bag. She always kept spares with her. She pulled out one she found. "This one's blue, and it will match your pretty dress."

"My dress is wrinkled," Jessica complained.

"Well, sometimes busy girls don't have time to iron dresses," Everly said. "Look at my shirt. See the wrinkles?"

Jessica nodded solemnly. Then she turned her head as Everly carefully brushed through the tangles. "Did you wash your hair last night?"

"Daddy made me."

Austin glanced over, his eyes wary, but Everly only smiled at him. His expression softened before he looked back at the road.

"After we get back to my place, I'm going to show your dad my most favorite conditioner to use," Everly soothed. "It won't make tangles in your hair."

"Okay," Jessica said in a small voice.

"Oh, and you can meet my kitty named Snatches."

Jessica's voice brightened. "You have a kitty?"

"I do, and she's very nice," Everly said. "She especially loves little girls who are seven."

Austin shook his head, but he was smiling.

"There, all done." Everly tucked the hair brush into her bag.

"That didn't even hurt," Jessica said, throwing her arms about Everly's waist.

"I'm so glad," Everly murmured, pulling her close.

Austin glanced over again, and for a moment their gazes held. Austin's brown eyes were full of gratitude, and Everly . . . she was grateful that Jessica's tears seemed to be a thing of the past.

All too soon, they pulled up to her mom's house. Everly immediately recognized Brock's SUV. She tried not to let her nerves get the better of her. She also recognized the car of one of her aunt and uncle's. Austin opened Jessica's door, and Everly slid out the same way.

"Thank you," Austin said, grasping her hand and squeezing. "Have I told you that you're amazing?"

He hadn't shaved this morning, and the scruff on his face combined with his chocolatey brown eyes made him very kissable. But Everly was pretty sure her mother at the very least was watching out the front window of the house. So, she settled for squeezing his hand back. "You might have, but I accept all compliments."

"Okay, then you're beautiful and amazing, and my daughter loves you."

The word *loves* might have sent the butterflies in her stomach into a tailspin, but Everly only smiled. "I'm good with that. Now, come on before my mother throws open the door."

As if on cue, the front door to her mom's house opened.

Austin only winked at her, then released her hand so he could rein in Jessica, who was climbing back into the truck because she forgot her Barbie. "Leave it in the truck, sweetie. We're not here to play."

"It's okay," Everly cut in. "I mean, no one will mind, if that's fine with you."

Austin hesitated, then shrugged. "Okay, Jessica. You can bring one."

"Hooray," Jessica said, snatching her doll, then beaming at Everly when she climbed out of the truck.

Sure enough, her mother stood in the entryway of the house, a wide smile on her face, although Everly wasn't fooled. Her mom was watching every movement and forming opinions of Austin and Jessica.

And . . . Aunt Janice and Uncle Stanley were present. Everyone crowded the living room to meet the new arrivals, so Everly made the introductions.

"Everyone, this is Austin Hayes and his daughter Jessica," she said. "And this is my sister Brandy, her fiancé, Brock, my aunt Janice, uncle Stanley, and my mom, Lydia."

She watched as Austin greeted everyone, shaking their hands, and she couldn't help comparing him to Brock as the two men exchanged short pleasantries. Brock's short blond hair and blue eyes were a contrast to Austin's dark hair and dark eyes. Brock was about an inch shorter yet broader than Austin. Everly knew first-hand how he spent one to two hours a day at the gym working on his sculpted physique. Austin was leaner, but more real to her.

Everly also caught Brandy sizing up the two men. Everly waited for Austin to notice her sister's beauty, to maybe gaze at her a moment too long, but he didn't seem affected. He simply shook her hand, smiled, then moved on. He came to stand next to Everly and linked their fingers.

Brock's gaze went to their linked hands, then moved back up. It had been subtle and quick, but Everly had noticed it. She had no idea what was going through Brock's mind, but she didn't care. She'd cried and agonized enough over how his smiles were now directed to her sister, how he could hardly keep his gaze off of her . . . yet, this morning, he was looking at Everly again as if he hadn't noticed her in a long, long time.

Everly refused to meet his gaze again, although that didn't mean she didn't feel it on her throughout the meal.

Jessica was perfectly polite and charming, and Everly's mom was sweet to her. A big relief. Brandy acted pleasant, but barely interacted with Jessica. Instead Brandy focused on Austin, asking him all sorts of questions about his job, his education.

"Are you divorced?" Aunt Janice asked.

Everly hadn't told her aunt about Austin specifically, but surely she knew . . .

"Widowed," Austin said simply.

"My mommy died," Jessica added in a matter-of-fact tone. "When I was five."

The table went absolutely silent, and Everly wanted to crawl into a hole.

"Oh, goodness," Aunt Janice said. "I'm very sorry to hear that." Her gaze shifted to Austin. "And you're already dating? That is so great."

Really? A hole right about now would be good. And Everly had been worried about her mom saying something awkward.

"Actually, Everly is the first woman I've dated since my wife's death," Austin said, his tone casual. "My mother would have liked me to be dating a lot sooner than now, but my career has been busy and I'd rather spend my nights and weekends with my daughter. Not only that, but no one had caught my eye until I came here. And now I don't know who likes Everly more, me or Jessica."

Everly was pretty sure she was blushing, and Brock and Brandy were definitely looking at her with interest.

"Oh, that's sweet," Aunt Janice said. "Everly always was a great babysitter."

"This salad dressing is really good, Mom," Everly said. "Is it homemade?"

Too obvious?

Her mom dragged her gaze away from Austin. When she met Everly's, she hoped her mom could see the pleading in her eyes. "Yes, in fact I found it on Pinterest. Which reminds me, I can't wait for you all to try my dessert. It's a new recipe. Jessica, do you like chocolate?"

And the conversation was finally diverted. Everly took another bite of her salad as Brandy talked about her charity work for African orphans and how Brock was putting together a trip for them later in the year to go visit some of the orphanages. His law firm was one of the top donors to Brandy's nonprofit.

"That is so wonderful," her mother said. "Such important work. Think of all those poor children over there with next to nothing."

Everly was starting to blank out, as she usually did when she was in the same room as Brandy and Brock. He'd never taken an interest in her art or any of her jobs. But with Brandy? He was putting resources from his law firm into hers.

It didn't matter. Not anymore. And then Everly felt another pair of eyes on her. She wondered what Austin thought of her family, or if he was ready to flee.

"You should come with us, Everly," Brandy said.

Everly lifted her gaze. She'd love to do a humanitarian project sometime, but with Brandy and Brock? No, thank you. "When you work out the details, I'll see what I can do," she said, because she was too weak to say no outright. Besides, she didn't want it to become a family discussion.

Brock then asked Austin about his dad's parents, and they figured out that his dad and Brock's dad were second cousins, which made Brock and Austin third or maybe fourth cousins? During the rest of the meal, Everly felt on edge, although everything seemed normal on the outside. On the inside, her mind raced, her stomach clenched, and she wanted to find a way to apologize to Austin for Janice's audacity.

Sixteen

AUSTIN WISHED THAT EVERLY WOULD talk to him as they drove back to her place. Well, she was talking, mostly to Jessica, but he knew there were things on Everly's mind that she wasn't saying. He could hear it in the higher pitch of her voice, and he could see it in the slight tremble of her hands. Right now, she and Jessica were talking about a Disney series that he'd never heard of. Something about wizards.

"Can we watch it together when I come back?" Jessica asked.

"That sounds fun," Everly said.

They were almost to Everly's place where they'd drop her off, then Austin would be taking Jessica back to his parents. She'd already protested, and asked to stay longer, but Everly had effectively calmed her down. She was good at that. And Austin appreciated it, but he also wished that he could have some alone time with Everly to find out what was really going on in that mind of hers.

It was pretty clear that being around Brock still rattled her. Thankfully, Austin didn't sense that she was attracted to him or anything, just that he was a giant elephant in the room. Brandy seemed nice, but overly analytical. Didn't she realize that Everly might need her space from Brock?

Austin could tell that Everly hadn't been happy with her aunt questioning him about Rachel. He'd been dealing with those questions for two years now. But after brunch, Everly had made it clear she didn't want to hang around her family any longer, and he was afraid that extended to him as well.

When he pulled around to the back of the craft store, Everly was already saying goodbye to Jessica and reaching for the door handle.

"Can I see your cat?" Jessica asked.

Austin felt Everly's hesitation, so he was surprised when she said, "Of course. And I need to show your dad my favorite conditioner, too."

Jessica beamed, and Austin would have normally felt the warm glow too, but Everly still hadn't met his gaze since the brunch.

Everly hopped out of the truck as soon as he parked, and Austin and Jessica followed her through the back door of the craft shop and up the stairs.

Meow.

The cat was waiting for them. "Hi, Snatches," Jessica crooned as Everly showed her how to hold the cat.

Then Jessica settled on the loveseat with the purring cat, and Everly brought out a purple bottle of conditioner.

"That's the stuff, huh?"

"Yep," Everly said in an overly bright tone. "Great for long hair."

He snapped a picture of it so that he wouldn't forget the name in case there were other purple bottles of conditioner in the store.

Then Everly joined Jessica on the loveseat, and together

they pet the cat. Austin slipped his hands into his pockets and gazed at the paintings on the walls, although his mind was far from the art. There was some sort of disconnect between Everly, and her mom and sister, and he couldn't quite put his finger on it.

He glanced over at Everly. Didn't she know how lovely and talented she was? He'd seen her practically shrink in the presence of her family as if her confidence had been a birthday candle, easily blown out.

Watching Everly and Jessica together made his heart expand in a way he hadn't ever thought possible. This weekend and been nothing short of enlightening. His questions about whether Jessica and the woman he was dating would mesh had been answered with a resounding *yes*. He was sure that Jessica would tell his parents all about Everly, and Austin had no doubt that his mom would have plenty of questions in the coming days and weeks.

"It's getting late, Jessica," Austin said.

"Aw, Dad, can we stay a little longer?" Jessica asked, her brown eyes full of pleading hope.

"We already have," Austin said, his gaze going to Everly's.

She was solely focused on the cat.

"Okay," Jessica said, then turned and hugged Everly.

When Everly drew away, she smiled. "Remember what I told you about the bracelets?"

"Don't let them get tangled up."

Everly nodded. "Exactly." She rose from the couch, and the cat darted into the kitchen to drink some water from a dish. "Be good for your dad on the drive home."

"I will," Jessica said in a cheerful voice.

"Jessica," Austin said. "Can you wait at the bottom of the stairs for a minute while I talk to Everly?"

Surprisingly, his daughter didn't argue or put up a fuss. She simply said, "Okay," and walked down the stairs. When Austin turned to look at Everly, she was folding her arms . . . not like she was mad, but more like she was protecting herself from something.

Austin moved closer, but she still didn't look at him.

"Everly," he said in a quiet voice and lifted her chin with the tips of his fingers. "Are you okay?"

His heart sank when he saw the tears forming in her eyes.

"I'm fine," she said. "And you've got to go. We can talk later."

Austin didn't like this one bit. But he really did need to start driving Jessica back home. "Do you want to ride with us? I know it's kind of a long drive, but I'd love for you to meet my parents."

Everly blinked, then blew out a shaky breath. "Not tonight, okay? I mean, I'm flattered you want to introduce me to your parents, but I've kind of had my fill of family for one day."

Austin moved his fingers along her jaw, then behind her neck. "I don't know why you underestimate yourself, but you do," he said, leaning his forehead against hers. "You need to stand your ground with your mom and sister. You don't always have to go along with everything they say just because they ask."

Everly broke their gaze. "I know, but it's complicated."

"I get it," he said. "Families are always complicated."

When she lifted her gaze, he saw a vulnerability that he both loved and hated. Loved because it meant she was willing to show him this side of her, and hated because he sensed she was keeping her pain to herself.

She wasn't pulling away though, so he kissed the edge of her mouth. He hated to see her hurting, or confused, or even not believing what he'd said about her at the brunch. "Everything I said at your mom's is true, you know. I haven't dated beyond a single night out since Rachel's death, and I still wouldn't be dating if I hadn't met you."

Nodding, she leaned into him, and he pulled her close. At last she was responding to him. He slid a hand around her waist, then to the small of her back. She wrapped her arms about his waist and tilted her head up. That was the only invitation he needed. He kissed her slowly, deliberately, and soon she warmed to him further. She kissed him back, sliding her hands up his back and anchoring him to her.

Soon, the kiss deepened as she pressed closer, and he sensed a fierceness welling up inside of her, almost a possessiveness. He cradled her face, kissing her like it had been a week since their last kiss, and truthfully, it had felt like that. "Don't go quiet on me, Everly," he whispered against her mouth.

"I won't," she whispered back.

He leaned his forehead against hers, willing his heart rate to return to normal. Willing his breathing to calm.

"Jessica's waiting," Everly murmured, her cheeks flushed.

"I'll call you on my drive back," Austin said.

"Okay," she murmured, her fingers skimming over his shoulders, then down his chest. "Drive safe."

"I will." Goosebumps had already raced across his skin, and now they multiplied. He kissed her again, lightly. Then, slowly, reluctantly, he released her. Every time he was with her, every time they were together, he didn't want to leave. She made his heart feel lighter, and she made him see that there was an entire existence beyond his past.

On the drive back to his parents, Jessica started to fall asleep. So, Austin had to do his best to keep her chattering, which ended up mostly about Barbie stuff and Disney stuff that he couldn't follow one-hundred percent. But he was sure his mother wouldn't appreciate Jessica coming home and staying up all hours of the night due to a nap.

He slowed the truck in front of his parents' home, then climbed out and helped Jessica get her things.

By the time they'd reached the porch, his dad had opened the door. Jessica flew into her grandpa's arms, and he chuckled and kissed the top of her head. "Do you have time to come in?" he asked Austin.

"Of course," he said, although he was pretty sure he'd be walking into an interrogation. He was right.

His mother was in the kitchen, cleaning out the pantry. She turned when she saw him, and he could see the trepidation in her eyes. But before they could speak, Jessica ran to her grandma and hugged her. His mom's face broke out into a smile.

Austin's heart tugged at the scene. His daughter was well-loved in this home, and he knew that if he changed things up, like moving to Everly Falls, it would crush his parents.

"Are you hungry?" his mom asked Jessica.

"I'm starving," she pronounced.

"We ate a big lunch," Austin said, but that was now hours ago. He didn't want his mom to think he hadn't fed Jessica.

His mom bustled about the kitchen putting together a sandwich and fruit for Jessica to eat.

"How was your trip?" she asked Jessica.

"It was so fun!" Jessica said. "Daddy has a girlfriend too."

Austin winced. He didn't mind the label, but coming from Jessica was probably not the right thing.

His mom cut a glance to him, then asked Jessica, "Do you like her?"

"Yes, and she knows all about Barbies." Jessica picked up her sandwich and took a bite. "She even likes to swing at the playground."

"Oh, she sounds quite . . . young."

"Who's young?" his dad asked, walking into the kitchen.

"Daddy's girlfriend. She's twenty," Jessica said.

"Twenty-seven," Austin corrected because now both of his parents were frowning.

"Oh. Twenty-seven." Jessica shrugged and took another bite.

"And she's never been married?" his mom asked in a quieter voice, this question directed at Austin.

"No," he said simply.

"We went on a hike to a waterfall," Jessica said. "I got to swim, but Daddy and Everly just watched. Did you know her last name is Kane? Like a queen and Kane, but she's a Kane." Jessica giggled. "Even though that's a boy's name."

Austin decided to jump in. "Tell Grandma and Grandpa about all the new friends you made."

So, Jessica proceeded to talk about Lizzy and the others. "And Lizzy is having a birthday party next weekend. Her birthday is the Fourth of July, but I want to go. Daddy said he has to talk to you."

His mom's surprised expression made Austin's throat turn into sandpaper.

"Right, we do need to discuss it, but not right now." He glanced over at his dad, who had a non-committal expression on his face.

"Do you even know Lizzy's family?" his mom asked.

Or . . . they could discuss it right now. "We got to know each other in the park," he said. "Everly knows the whole family. It's a small town and all."

"We planned to go to the parade in the morning of the Fourth, then the fair later in the day," his mom said, her tone sounding pouty. "The fireworks are supposed to be bigger this year than last year."

Austin nodded. "Right."

"All done," Jessica announced. Then, as she'd been taught, she rose from the table and cleared her plate and cup.

"So, this Everly woman, she's *from* Everly Falls?" his dad asked.

"She is," Austin confirmed. "Her mom and sister live there too."

"She's named after her town," Jessica announced. "And her dad died. Like my mom died, but I was five, and Everly was bigger."

"That's too bad," his mom soothed. "Sorry to hear that."

"And Daddy holds both of our hands," Jessica continued. "It's funny."

Austin stilled.

"Oh, that's nice," his mom continued, although her voice was strained. "Can you come help me with something in the other room, Austin?"

It had been her ruse growing up when she wanted to have a private conversation with his dad. And now he was the selected.

He followed her down the hall while his dad and Jessica were still in the kitchen. His mom stepped into the office-slash-craft room, then turned with folded arms. "How serious are you with this woman?"

Austin exhaled. "We've only been dating a couple of weeks."

His mom wasn't fooled. "Things can happen fast, especially with young people nowadays. I've heard all about the bed-hopping."

"There's been no bed-hopping, mom," he said, shocked at her accusation. It was none of her business anyway. Well, it shouldn't be. With Jessica in her fulltime care this summer, things were more delicate than he had control over. "Don't insult a woman you've never even met."

His mom looked duly chagrined, but her eyes now swam with tears. "I don't want Jessica hurt. You're working a temporary job, that's all, Austin. There's no reason for you to throw a wrench into everything."

Austin hadn't wanted to get into the discussion this deeply yet, especially when he knew that Everly was struggling with her own family. And Austin honestly didn't know what their future held. Together or apart. He didn't have any answers right now.

"I understand where you're coming from," he said in a quiet tone. "But Everly Kane is a wonderful person. I haven't been dating since Rachel because there hadn't been any women who'd captured my attention."

"And Everly has now captured your attention?"

"Correct."

His mom looked away and brushed at the tears on her face. "You have to think about Jessica, too."

"I am, believe me," Austin said, although he felt conflicted right now. His mother's pain and uncertainty were things he'd also experienced. "This weekend was good for that. Everly and Jessica get along fine. And that doesn't mean that everything will be peachy all of the time, but it was a good thing to help me know for sure."

"Know what for sure?"

"That I want to continue dating Everly," he said. "I don't know where it will lead, Mom. It's too early to know. Yet I want you to know that Jessica will always be the most important person in my life. No one else will ever change that."

His mom nodded, seeming satisfied.

But he wasn't finished. "And I know this is hard to hear, but I need to say it. I think there's more that I can offer Jessica. A real home, and not an apartment. A neighborhood where there are kids her age to play with after school."

His mother pursed her lips. Their circumstances weren't ideal, but Jessica was loved and cared for, and he was sure his mom would take offense to what he was saying. But it had to be said.

"I'm stronger now than I was in the months after Rachel's illness and death," he said, taking courage from his own words. "I'm looking toward the future now and not surviving a day at a time. You've been wonderful to us, and I'll never be able to repay you. But I'd like to buy a home, get established, and feel human again."

His mom's tears had started anew.

"I don't know where I'll get a house," he said. "It might be somewhere close to you, it might be . . . in Everly Falls. I don't know, but I want you to know that change is coming. Even if things with Everly don't progress, I'm ready for progression myself. And I think Jessica is too."

His mom wiped at her cheeks, then sniffled. Lifting her chin, she said, "All right, Son, I understand. I want you to know that your decisions affect more than just you and Jessica."

Austin's own eyes burned with emotion. "I know, Mom. And I love you and Dad, and I'm not going to blindside you. Believe me, I'm not making any of these decisions lightly."

His mom snatched a tissue from a tissue box on the desk and dabbed at her face. Austin crossed to her and pulled her into his arms.

Leaning into him, his mom said, "I guess we'd better meet this Everly woman."

Austin nodded. "How about you and dad make a trip to Everly Falls next weekend? I can get you a room at the bed and breakfast. We'll enjoy the Fourth of July festivities as a family. Then you can meet Everly for yourself, and offer your advice as well."

His mother chuckled. "You want my advice?"

"I do want it," he said with his own smile. "I don't know if I'll take it, but I want it nonetheless."

His mom drew back, and he was relieved to see her smile up at him. "All right, change is always hard, but I know you need to move on from Rachel, too. Her death has affected all of us, and I'm proud of you for being such a great dad through it all."

By the time Austin left his parents' home, he was feeling great. He called Everly on his Bluetooth, but she didn't answer. When he tried an hour later, she still didn't answer.

Seventeen

WHEN EVERLY OPENED HER EYES, it was still dark. Then she realized she'd fallen asleep after Austin left. More like cried herself to sleep. And now it was eleven at night, and she was wide awake with a throbbing headache. She slowly climbed out of bed and made her way to the kitchen in the dark, only the moonlight acting as a guide.

Snatches had gone somewhere through the kitchen window. Probably enjoying whatever her second night life was. Everly located some ibuprofen and downed it with a glass of water. Then she climbed back into bed, turned on the lamp by her bed, and picked up her phone. She'd missed two calls from Austin and a text: *Just got back. Call me if you're still awake.*

The text was over two hours old.

Everly could talk to him tomorrow. The nap had calmed her emotions, and now that she looked back on the brunch at her mom's, things didn't seem too bad. Brandy had been nice when she invited her on the Africa trip. Everly had told her more than once that being around Brock didn't bother her, so why would Brandy think any different?

141

Austin had handled her aunt Janice with aplomb, and his sweet words about Everly being the first woman he'd been interested in dating had seemed genuine. Especially when he'd kissed her later on.

It was almost like Austin was too good to be true. Did that mean he was? Was she simply wearing rose-colored glasses? Had she read too much into Austin's casual questions about her town and assumed they had more meaning than they really did?

Had her affinity with Jessica only been first-time luck? And the next time around, would things start to clash between them when the newness wore off?

Maybe Everly should turn off the light and go back to sleep. Before she could, her phone rang. Her heart skipped a couple beats as she anticipated Austin calling again. But it wasn't Austin. It was a number she had once blocked, but then unblocked when her sister got engaged.

Brock Hayes.

For a moment, Everly was too stunned to decide if she wanted to answer the phone. By the third ring she was so curious she just picked it. Besides, maybe it was Brandy, calling from Brock's number for some reason?

"Eve?" Brock said. He was the only one who'd ever called her that, and the host of memories it brought twisted uncomfortably in her belly.

"Hi, Brock," she said, knowing her tone sounded breathless.

"How are you?"

This was not what she expected. Why didn't he get right to the point? "I'm fine."

"Still a night owl?" he said with increasing familiarity, as if it were their own inside joke.

"I actually just woke up," she said. "I took a late nap, I

guess." Why was she telling him any of this? And where was Brandy? She was probably snuggled next to him, listening in. "What are you and Brandy up to?"

"Brandy's home," Brock said. "I couldn't sleep." His voice was lower now, and it sent a shiver of warning through her. Why, she had no idea.

"Oh, are you sick or something?"

His chuckle was low. "I'm fine, Eve. I wanted to ask you more about this guy you're dating. I mean, what do you really know about him?"

Everly was too surprised to answer at first.

"I could come over for a few, if you want," Brock offered. "You know, if it's easier to talk in person. I'm kind of concerned about you jumping into this. He has a kid and everything. That's a huge commitment."

She sat straight up in bed. First of all, she had no problem with commitment. She was twenty-seven, and dating a guy who had a kid was probably going to be a common thing, even if she and Austin didn't stay together.

"Is that why you're calling, Brock?" she asked, feeling annoyed and hot at the same time. "To warn me off dating Austin?"

"Look," he soothed, which only felt condescending to her. "You're a smart woman, Eve. I think that you've been through a lot of things, and changes, so you might not be thinking straight. In this case anyway."

"Did Brandy ask you to call me?"

"No," Brock said quickly. "And I prefer to keep this conversation between ourselves."

Well, that sent up a red flag, and Everly wasn't going to play whatever game Brock thought he could talk her into playing. "I don't keep secrets from Brandy, so you'd better get used to that, especially if you're going to be my brother-in-law. Besides, why would it be a secret in the first place?"

He didn't answer for a moment, then he said in slow voice, "Did you ever wonder what might have happened if we'd stayed together?"

Everly was dumbfounded. *He'd* broken up with *her.* "Not anymore," she said. "Maybe I did a while ago, but I can honestly say that I'm glad we parted ways. You and Brandy are perfect together."

Another silence on his end, then he said, "I wouldn't say *perfect.*"

"Don't be that guy, Brock Hayes," she said in a voice probably too sharp, but she no longer cared. She couldn't even sit anymore. She paced her small apartment. "You're engaged to the most amazing woman in the world. My sister deserves the best, and if you can't be the best, then—"

"Whoa, Eve, calm down."

Which of course only made her madder. "And stay out of *my* business. I don't care if you're going to be my brother-in-law soon, you have no right to tell me what to do or who to date. And calling me without Brandy knowing is inappropriate. So I'm hanging up now, and I'll also be letting my sister know about this call—"

"Eve, wait, please," Brock said, his tone pleading. "Whether or not you tell Brandy won't change the fact that I called to warn you off Austin. You don't know the guy. He's an outsider, and he comes with a lot of baggage."

Everly closed her eyes against Brock's words. He had no right . . .

"Come on, Eve," Brock continued. "Do you think I'd call you up if I wasn't truly concerned? I mean, I *know* you . . . you know me. We used to be best friends, and I thought we were pretty good together."

Everly's laugh was bitter. "I don't even know your point, Brock. *You* broke up with *me*, remember?"

"I know," he said. "But it wasn't because I didn't care about you. It was because I knew you were the real deal, and I guess that I wasn't ready to be serious with anyone. To fully commit. And I knew that you wanted to settle down, and I didn't want to lead you on."

This was not at all what she expected to hear.

"But you jumped in with two feet with Brandy," she said. "You *proposed* to her, and you're getting married now."

"I finally grew up," he said in a low tone. "Decided to be a man."

Everly rubbed at her temples, wondering if her headache would ever go away. "Well, congratulations, and I hope you do the right thing for once."

"The thing is, Eve . . ." he said.

Her heartrate spiked. *Don't say it, Brock. Don't you dare.*

"I miss you."

Everly's breath stalled. "I'm going to pretend you didn't say that, Brock. And I'm going to hope to all that is holy that you pull your head out of the gutter and realize how amazing Brandy is and how much she loves you."

Tears streaked Everly's cheeks now, but she wasn't finished. "If you ever call me again, for any reason, I'll tell Brandy about every single word you said tonight. As of now, I'm telling her that you called and warned me against Austin, and that I didn't appreciate it. The rest is between the two of you. I've moved on, Brock. With or without Austin, I've moved on."

Before he could answer, she hung up. She composed a long text to Brandy because she knew if she called her instead, she'd only cry. Then she pressed send. If Brandy was asleep, then she'd see it in the morning. She and Brock would have to work out their own relationship.

Then she sent a text Austin. *Are you awake?*

He wrote back instantly. *Yes.*

She pushed send on his number. When he answered, the tears started full force again. Embarrassment shot through her, but she managed to drag in a full breath and talk semi-normally. The warm depths of his voice were a soothing balm. "Sorry I didn't answer earlier. I took a nap."

"I'm sure you needed that nap," he said.

She closed her eyes, letting his low tones wash over her. "I think I did."

"Do you feel better now?"

"Um, yes, and no." And then she told him about Brock's phone call and how Brock had said he missed her.

Austin's response wasn't what she expected. "What did you tell him?"

"I told him to never contact me again." She exhaled. "I also sent a text to my sister about his call. Brock is so far in my past, that I barely remember us together. And even if I wasn't dating you, I would never go back to him."

"I think he needs to figure out his life," Austin said. "But clearly he still likes you."

"He has cold feet," Everly said. "He and Brandy . . . they're like two peas in a pod."

"Maybe," he agreed, "But I'm glad you told Brandy about the call. If there are potential issues, she needs to know as well."

"Yeah," Everly said, her mind still spinning.

"Do you want me to talk to him?"

"No, I think that would just make it into a bigger deal," she said. "And I want it to be over on my end."

"Okay," he said. "Are you going to be okay, or do you need some company?"

When Brock had asked her that, she'd been repulsed, but with Austin . . . She was tempted. "I don't think it's a good idea. I wouldn't let you leave."

"I wouldn't mind," he teased.

And she found herself smiling.

"Or you could come over here," he said. "I have leftover snacks from Jessica's visit."

"So tempting." She laughed. "How was the drive, by the way? Did you manage to keep her awake?"

"I did," Austin said. "She was happy to see her grandparents, that's for sure, but it didn't curb her begging to come back next weekend for the Fourth."

Everly settled back onto her bed and pulled one of her pillows against her chest. "So, are you going to bring her?" *Say yes.*

"I hope so," he said. "I brought it up with my parents— my mom more specifically. I invited them as well."

Everly raised her brows. "Oh, really? That would be great." Her heart was hammering for some reason. If Austin had his parents visiting the town, she'd meet them for sure. And then she wondered what his motivation was in all of this . . . She could only dare to hope it might have something to do with going to the next level in their relationship.

"So, what are you doing tomorrow night?"

"Hanging out with you?"

"Good answer."

She grinned and burrowed into her covers. She could listen to Austin's voice all night. "What are we doing tomorrow night, Mr. Architect?"

"I thought I'd come by your place, pick you up, and take you to the movies."

"It's Monday tomorrow," she said. "My movie night is Wednesday."

"Maybe you could try something different," he said. "With me."

Warm tingles spread across her arms. "Hmm, what's playing?"

"I don't even know."

Everly laughed. "All right, I'm in."

"Perfect answer," he said again, and she heard the smile in his voice. "I'm glad you called, Everly."

She exhaled. "I'm glad you answered."

"Good night," he said. "See you soon."

Everly didn't sleep for a while after that. Nope. With the combination of a rather long day, a late nap, Brock's annoying call, then the butterfly-inducing one to Austin, her thoughts were all over the place.

It was only when Snatches decided to reappear at the window and leap onto her bed, that Everly finally drifted off to sleep.

Eighteen

"MY SISTER'S NOT EVEN SPEAKING to me right now," Everly told Austin over the phone.

He was on his way to pick her up for their movie night. They'd texted a couple of times throughout the day, but he sensed that Everly was being reserved, and now he knew why.

"What did your mom say?" he asked, wondering if this had become a family issue.

"I haven't said anything to her," Everly said. "But Brandy might have. I don't know. She called me this morning and basically accused me of making up the scenario of Brock's intentions when he called. I guess he told her a different version, and she's going to believe him."

"I'm not surprised that Brock has a different version, but the question is what are you going to do about it?"

"Nothing," Everly said with a sigh. "I mean, I told Brandy what I needed to. And now I'm going to stay out of it. Except her wedding is in ten days, and I feel bad about this all happening right now."

"You've done nothing wrong," Austin said. "Unless

dating *me* is the real issue here, or maybe Brock is getting cold feet about his wedding and realizing what he gave up in you."

Everly groaned. "I really, really hope that's not true. And, Austin, my sister is going to have to get used to me dating a real person."

Austin chuckled as he turned into the parking lot and pulled around to the back of the craft store. The sun had set, but there was still plenty of light coming from the gold and orange horizon. "Good." His tone sobered. "And your sister should know that starting off a marriage with regrets is the wrong thing to do. Believe me, I know."

Her tone was curious when she asked, "Did that happen with Rachel?"

"Yeah," he said. "Hey, I'm at the shop. Do you want me to come up?"

"No, I'm ready," she said, "I'll come down."

He climbed out of the truck anyway, and walked to the back entrance to wait for her. When the door opened, he smiled at Everly.

She was wearing a green blouse with white jeans. Her hair was down tonight, settling about her shoulders in tawny-gold waves. She looked as pretty as a summer morning.

"Hi," she said, her lips curving into a smile, lips that looked extra pink.

"You're a sight for sore eyes," he said.

"Oh really?" She stepped into his arms.

"Really." He slipped his hands about her waist and pulled her close. Then he buried his face in the crook of her neck, breathing her in for a moment. Her body fit against his like a dream, and she smelled like heaven.

After a long moment, in which he made no move to release her, she said against his ear, "You know, I saw you yesterday."

"I know."

He felt her smile as she softly threaded her fingers through his hair. When she drew away, her hazel eyes were filled with warmth as she gazed at him. Warmth and questions. "Tell me about what you regretted, Austin."

He should have known she'd ask this. Reaching for her hand, he drew her to the truck, then opened the door for her. She climbed in, and when he settled into the driver's seat, he said, "We'd had a lot of ups and downs, and we'd completely broken up twice. I pretty much proposed because she gave me an ultimatum. Well, technically it was her parents."

"Wow, that's kind of crazy," Everly said as they pulled out of the parking lot. "And you felt stuck?"

"More than stuck," he said. "She'd had a pregnancy scare that turned out to not be positive, but her parents were adamant that we tie the knot. I loved her, sure, but I wasn't ready to commit to something so big and permanent. And it turned out later that she wasn't either."

He felt Everly's sympathetic gaze on him. He wasn't looking for sympathy though. Reaching for Everly's hand, he loved how it felt so natural, so easy, to hold her hand. It was like they'd known each other much longer than a few weeks. In fact, it was hard to remember his life before Everly was in it.

"Did you ever suspect Rachel was unfaithful?" she asked.

"Oh, the signs were there, but I didn't want to recognize them," he said. "I mean, we had a kid together, one we both adored. To me, being unfaithful would have been an insult to my daughter as well."

Everly rubbed her thumb slowly over his knuckles. "You're a good man, Austin Hayes."

He slowed the truck at the final light before the theater and leaned over to give her a barely-there kiss.

She smiled against his lips, and when he lifted his head, she added, "See, you just proved my point."

The light turned green, and he accelerated the truck. "Well, you're a good sister, daughter, and girlfriend."

"Oh, is that what I am now, your girlfriend?" she teased.

He glanced over at her. "You'd better be."

She leaned across the seat and kissed his cheek. "I'm good with that."

"Good, because that's what Jessica told my parents."

He felt her surprise rather than saw it.

"So, if they come out this weekend, they'll think I've already stolen you from them?"

She didn't know how close to the truth she was hitting with that statement. "They're going to love you. Trust me."

Everly said nothing, but leaned her head against his shoulder. He decided he liked her sitting this close to him. As they pulled into the parking lot, there were about a half dozen cars there.

"See," she said. "Wednesday nights are better."

Austin only grinned. They walked into the theater, and he bought the popcorn and drinks. Since there was only one theater open right now, they only had one movie choice.

"What if my favorite seats are taken?" she asked as they walked into the theater room. The lights had already dimmed.

"I saved the row."

"The entire row?"

"Shh, the movie's about to start."

Everly gave a soft laugh as they entered the main part of the theater. By the light of the preview they made their way to the center row, where it was sectioned off with yellow construction tape.

Austin snapped the tape in half, then motioned for her to step into the row first. He followed, and sure enough she picked the very center seat, so his seat next to her was one off center.

The movie started after the next preview, and Everly slid down in her seat.

"What are you doing?" Austin whispered.

"Getting comfortable," she said. "Also, you can only eat one piece of popcorn at a time."

"Good thing I'm not hungry then."

She smirked, and he slid down in his seat, matching her posture, then he took out one piece of popcorn from her tub and ate it.

"So fulfilling."

"Shh," she said. "The movie's started."

He only grinned, then leaned close and pressed his mouth against her neck.

She squirmed, then giggled.

"That tickles," she whispered. "Haven't you shaved recently?"

"No," he whispered back, then he kissed her earlobe.

"Stop, I can't focus."

"I'll stop when the movie starts."

She set the popcorn tub on the floor, then turned toward him. Lifting her hand to his jaw, she slowly traced her fingers along his stubble. "Okay, you can kiss me until the movie starts. But then you have to stop."

"Yes, ma'am." He closed the distance and pressed his mouth against hers.

Her hand slid around his neck as she kissed him back. She tasted warm and smelled of buttery popcorn.

"I feel like a teenager," she whispered against his mouth.

"Me too." He wanted to tug her onto his lap, to pull her closer, to get lost in their kissing.

But the opening notes of the movie's music score played,

and Everly drew back. She set the popcorn between them. He groaned, but she only smiled and turned her attention to the giant movie screen.

Austin couldn't exactly say he was watching the action flick, because he was so aware of each movement and reaction from Everly. He loved how invested she became in the movie; it reminded him of his daughter. It was like she became part of the movie, reacting to all the ups and downs of the film.

At the end of it, when all the good guys prevailed over the bad guys, she clapped along with the others in the audience.

"Oh, so you're one of those," he whispered.

She turned her gaze on him. "One of what?"

"Those people who clap at the end of the movie, then watch the credits."

She only smiled, then once again ignored him in favor of watching names of producers and actors and crew scrolling up the screen.

Austin could be patient. He wasn't going anywhere. At least not tonight.

When the final credits rolled, and the music faded, they were the only ones left in the theater.

"Now, can I kiss you?" Austin teased.

Everly rolled her eyes. "You have a one-track mind. Did you even watch the movie, or were you watching me the whole time?"

"Guilty."

She laughed, then gathered the empty popcorn tub and added their drink cups inside. "Come on so you don't fall asleep in here."

He grasped her hand, and she tugged him to his feet, although he didn't really need help. He was only too happy to stand and pull her close. Leaning down, he brushed his mouth against hers.

"Come on, Mr. Architect," she whispered. "We're going to get locked in."

"I don't mind," he murmured, kissing her again.

But Everly seemed to have the willpower of Superman, and she drew away, then tugged his hand and led him out of the row.

"Do you want me to take you home, or do you want to go for a walk at the park?" he asked as they headed outside to his truck. The summer night air was perfectly warm, and Austin was far from tired.

"A walk sounds nice," Everly said, squeezing his hand.

"Okay, great." He drove to the park. When they parked, they climbed out of the truck and walked the perimeter, hand in hand. It was after nine, so the place was hopping with teens at the skate park. They even populated the playground, running around, having fun.

"Oh no," Everly said, looking down at her phone.

"What is it?"

"My mom called three times, and she texted me to call her asap."

Austin didn't miss the alarm in her voice. "Call her then. I can take you over to her house if you want."

"I'll call." Everly pressed send on her phone.

Austin couldn't hear everything that was said, but he caught enough of Everly's side of the conversation to know that there'd been some sort of blow up between Brandy and Brock, and Brandy had taken off.

They'd reached the far side of the park where things were quieter. Austin noticed a lone person sitting on one of the benches. As they drew closer, it became obvious it was a woman. Her straight blonde hair reminded him of Brandy.

"Everly," Austin said, cutting into her conversation with her mom. "I think Brandy's over there."

Everly paused and looked over. "Mom. I've gotta go. Brandy's at the park. I'll talk to her, then call you." She hung up with a sigh.

"Did they break up?" Austin asked in a quiet voice.

"I'm not sure, and my mom's not sure," Everly said, blinking rapidly, her voice trembling. "But things aren't good."

Austin rubbed her back, trying to soothe her. "Talk to your sister. This is a bump in the road."

"You don't understand," Everly said. "Their fight was about *me*."

Austin stared at her. "About . . . his phone call?"

She drew in a shaky breath. "There was more, I guess. Brock told her he wasn't completely over me. He didn't realize it until I showed up at the brunch last Sunday with you."

Nineteen

SOMETIMES EVERLY HATED THE HARD things in life, and this was one of those instances. Her sister's huddled form on the bench told her that Brandy's heart had been broken. By the same man who'd broken her own. Who better to offer comfort? The dark irony tasted bitter on her tongue.

Maybe Brock just had cold feet. There was no way that he still had feelings for Everly. She'd witnessed the progression of the relationship between him and Brandy. He adored her, and she adored him.

But as she walked toward the lone figure of her sister on the park bench, the doubts plagued Everly. Brock had called her last night, and he'd said things that weren't normal for a man who was in love with his fiancée.

"Brandy?" she said in a quiet voice.

Her sister lifted her head in surprise, then her entire body tensed. "What are you doing here?"

"Austin and I were on a walk."

Brandy glanced over at Austin, who was keeping his distance. Her makeup was streaked, giving no doubt that she'd been crying.

"Mom called me," Everly added.

Brandy sniffled. "Did she tell you that Brock and I broke up?"

Everly held back a gasp. "She said that you guys were in a fight . . . I didn't know it was that serious."

"He told me he's not over you," Brandy said, then she began to cry.

"I'm so sorry," Everly whispered, sitting next to her sister. "I think he's confused. I know he loves you. I mean, he broke up with me. And yeah, it took me a while to get over him, but when I saw the two of you together . . . I knew you guys had the real thing."

Brandy wiped at the tears on her face. "It doesn't matter if he loves me, because it's not enough. I can't marry a man who can't make up his mind."

Everly's belly ached. She scooted over and pulled Brandy into her arms.

"I've felt so guilty for so long," Brandy said, her voice shaky as she leaned against Everly. "And that's gone now. Weird, huh? I didn't realize what a burden that had been."

Everly rubbed her sister's back. "You never had to feel guilty."

"I did anyway," Brandy said. "And I can't believe how supportive you've been. I don't think I could have ever done that."

"I did it because I love you more than anything."

Brandy exhaled then lifted her head. "I'm leaving tomorrow," she said. "Mom doesn't know yet, but I'm canceling everything in the morning. Then I'm getting in my car and driving someplace. I don't know where yet, and I don't know what I'm going to do. But I need to get out of this town for a bit. The gossiping will be like wild fire."

Everly's eyes stung, but she nodded, knowing that her sister needed time and healing.

"Can I ask you a favor?" Brandy whispered.

"Of course, anything," she said.

"Can you be there for Mom? She's going to take it hard."

"I can," Everly said.

"You know how she is with her daughters getting married," Brandy said, her tone ironic. "She'll probably try to talk me into marrying Brock after all."

Everly nodded. This was true.

"But I'm taking comfort in knowing that you found your Mr. Right," Brandy said. "That should keep Mom off my case when I go on a very long relationship hiatus."

"Mr. Right?" Everly said. "I don't know about that. Things are still pretty new with Austin."

Brandy patted Everly's knee. "Well, I'm calling it like I see it, big sister."

Everly smirked, and the two women embraced.

"Go to him," Brandy said, squeezing Everly tight. "I'm going to be fine. I'm sitting here planning my bright and glorious future."

"Are you sure?"

Brandy drew away and offered a brave smile. "I'm sure."

"Mom wants me to call her," Everly said. "I told her I saw you in the park."

"I'll call her," Brandy said. "I owe her the truth. It's the only way we can move forward, and I don't want her trying to convince me to give Brock a second chance."

"Good plan." Everly hugged her sister again, then rose to her feet. "Keep me posted on your travels. And stay safe."

"I will."

Everly crossed the grass in the moonlight, walking toward Austin.

"Will she be okay?" he asked in a quiet voice.

"She will be," Everly said. "She's canceling all the wedding stuff tomorrow, then going on a solo trip."

"Does she need help with anything?" he asked, sliding his hand over her shoulder.

"She'll let me know," Everly said, grasping his hand and linking their fingers. "Right now, she wants to be alone."

Austin moved his thumb over her wrist in the way that she loved.

"You were right, Austin," Everly said. "Brock told her he wasn't over me, and she can't very well marry a man she can't trust. I don't know if I believe Brock since I don't think he knows his own heart and mind. But all of this makes me appreciate you more." She stepped closer to him and placed a hand on his chest. "Thanks for not being a jerk."

His mouth lifted at the corners, and he drew her close, his fingers stroking her back in gentle circles. "You're welcome."

Everly hated that her sister was so sad. But she supposed that it was better to find out Brock's true nature before the wedding instead of after.

After Austin took her home that night, she and Brandy exchanged a few texts. Everly said to send her a to-do list of things to cancel so that Brandy wouldn't have to make the phone calls. And then her mom called. It was late, but it seemed none of the Kane women would be getting much sleep tonight.

"I want to burn his place down," her mom said first thing. "Tonight. Do you want to come with me?"

Everly was so shocked that she laughed. "Am I driving, or are you?"

"You'd better drive," her mom said. "I might speed, and we'll get pulled over. I don't think I can talk Officer Carlton into letting me off the hook again. No matter how in love that man is with his new woman."

"Officer Carlton would be the least of our concerns if we have arson materials in the trunk."

Her mom sighed. "I hate him right now. But I'm also relieved. If this is Brock's true nature, I don't want him married to either one of my daughters."

Everly matched her mom's sigh. "I agree. I hate that everything went so far with the wedding plans, but maybe it's a blessing in disguise."

"Right..." her mom's voice trailed off. "I'll have my black clothes and can of gasoline on standby though. I'm only a phone call away."

Everly smiled. "Thanks, Mom. I'm glad you're not brushing this under the rug and telling Brandy to give him a second chance."

"Never," her mom said, her tone steely. "That man doesn't deserve Brandy. Or you."

Everly closed her eyes and exhaled. "I hope the fallout won't be too hard on Brandy."

"People in town need to mind their own business." Her mom released a heavy sigh. "We'll get through this. The Kane women always do."

"Yep," Everly said. "I told Brandy I'd make calls for her tomorrow, and she told me to watch over you."

"I have the best daughters," her mom said, her voice full of emotion. "And I'm happy for you and Austin. If he's around this coming weekend, bring him for our brunch."

"Okay, Mom," Everly said. "His parents might come for the Fourth of July celebrations."

"The more the merrier," her mom said. "It's not like I have a wedding to get ready for."

Everly laughed, even though she didn't mean to. But her mom started laughing as well until Everly had tears in her eyes from laughing so hard. When they hung up, Everly was still smiling. Her mother was right. The Kane women would be fine.

The next few days sped by as Everly deflected questions about Brandy and Brock at the craft store, which had apparently become a gossip center. She spent her evenings with Austin, and that was always the best part of her day. He even included her in his nightly phone calls with Jessica. It was cute hearing her sweet voice through the phone, and more than once Austin excused himself to work on something while Everly and Jessica went deep into their conversations about the world of fairies or Barbies.

On Friday afternoon, Everly was a bundle of nerves though. Austin's parents would arrive early in the evening with Jessica. It wasn't that Everly wasn't looking forward to meeting them, but she was nervous all the same. This was definitely a big step in her relationship with Austin.

Not only that, but he said he had a surprise for her sometime that weekend. He just didn't know when it would be exactly.

Whatever thoughts had been tumbling about in her mind immediately dissipated when Brock Hayes walked into the craft shop. Unless he was on an errand for his mom, Brock was here to see Everly.

From her position at the end of one of the aisles that she was restocking with vanilla scented candles, she watched him talk to Darla. Darla promptly pointed Everly out, and Brock nodded. Then started walking toward her.

Everly wanted to disappear. To turn and hurry down the aisle and continue straight out the back door. What was Brock thinking? Yeah, she'd blocked him, so maybe he'd tried to text or call? That was his giant hint to not contact her. Yet, he was striding toward her like he was a man on a mission. His blond hair was tousled, his blue eyes looked strained and red, and his dress shirt that he probably wore to the office was half-untucked. In short, she'd never seen Brock Hayes this undone.

Everly folded her arms as he approached. Thankfully, the store wasn't crowded at the moment, but that wouldn't stop the town's gossip from spreading.

"Where is she?" Brock asked.

Everly didn't need him to clarify who he was asking about. "She went out of town."

Brock exhaled, then scrubbed a hand through his already messy hair. "I screwed up, Eve."

"You think?" She took a step into the aisle. Darla was glancing over at them with curiosity.

Brock took the hint and followed. "I didn't mean . . . I didn't think . . ." His gaze landed on the floor. "I wanted to be honest because Brandy is so pure, I was feeling guilty. Conflicted, too. Can you talk to her for me? Tell her I'm sorry. She can cancel the wedding if she wants, but I want another chance. I don't want us to be over."

When his blue eyes met hers, Everly felt the tiniest bit of compassion.

"We're sisters, Brock," she said in a hushed tone. "She's more important to me than anything you're feeling. Besides, the wedding is already cancelled. Did you think she was kidding? No woman should ever be second choice, especially my sister."

Brock closed his eyes and rubbed a hand over his face. When he looked at her again, she was a bit gratified to see the tears there. He deserved to cry. He'd been awful. "I'm so sorry. I don't know why . . . I guess seeing you with Austin brought back some memories, and it threw me for a loop."

"A big loop apparently."

Brock grimaced.

"Look, you need to leave," Everly said. "I'm not going to be in the middle of anyone's relationship, especially yours."

Brock nodded, although the lines on his forehead told her he was far from happy about her refusal to talk to him.

Everly walked down the aisle and turned into the next one. Brock remained in the first aisle for a few moments, then he headed out of the store. Everly knew it would be a while before any of them got full closure on this whole situation. But she was more than ready to have Brock Hayes fully and permanently out of her life.

When her phone buzzed with a text, she pulled it out of her craft apron pocket. Austin had texted: *2 hours.*

Meaning, two hours until he picked her up, and they went to meet his parents. She was more than ready. Yeah, she'd be nervous, but if Austin wanted her to meet Mr. and Mrs. Hayes, she was all in.

Twenty

AUSTIN PACED THE HOTEL LOBBY. His parents still hadn't shown up, and he hadn't heard from either of them for an hour. He'd texted both his mom and dad, but nothing. It was times like this that he wished Jessica had a cell phone, even if she was only seven years old. What if something had delayed them? What if there'd been an accident?

The knots in his stomach only tightened as the scenarios ran through his mind. He'd already let Everly know that everything was running late. He wished she was here now, but there was also prudence in talking to his parents for a few moments when they arrived, without Everly around.

Because he was about to deliver news that might stun them.

It was part of his surprise for Everly, and hopefully Jessica would be excited about it. He'd spent most of the day looking at properties. Condos, apartments, older homes, newer homes, and he'd found something that he knew would be perfect. It was actually down the block from Lizzy's family, and if Jessica and Lizzy stayed friends, they'd only be four houses apart from each other.

As it was, Lizzy's birthday party started in thirty minutes, and Austin was pretty sure that Jessica would throw a royal fit if she missed it.

But safety was more important.

When the tan-colored mini-van pulled up to the motel, Austin nearly sprinted out of the lobby doors. His parents drove a mini-van because his mom was always hauling stuff around for this and that.

He grinned as his mom and dad climbed out, and Jessica rushed to meet him.

"Hey, sweetie," he said, crushing her against him. "I've been waiting for you."

"Can you take me to Lizzy's?" she asked. "Grandma doesn't know the way, and she and Grandpa said they have to check into their room."

"Of course," Austin said, his gaze connecting with his parents. "I'll be back soon, and then we can meet up with Everly."

He didn't miss the slight pursing of his mother's lips. He had hoped that she would have warmed up to the idea by now. If not, his announcement would be all that harder to swallow down. On the short ride to Lizzy's home, he slowed as he passed the home with the For Sale sign in front of it. The neighborhood was quiet, and even in the glow of twilight, it looked inviting and cozy—something he never thought he'd look for in a house. But now with a seven-year-old daughter, and possibly more children in the future, it was a priority.

Soon they were at Lizzy's, and it turned out that Jessica was right on time. Austin greeted both of Lizzy's parents, then hovered in the entry way, watching Jessica chatter excitedly with Lizzy and two other kids.

"She'll do great," Brad said. "You're welcome to stay or come pick her up in two hours."

Austin nodded. He'd never taken Jessica to a birthday party before where the parents left. *It will be okay*, he told himself. "Great, I'll be back at the end. You have my cell if you need anything."

"We do," Brad said with a nod.

Then Austin was on his way back to the hotel to pick up his parents. They were in the lobby when he pulled up. They came out and climbed in to the truck, his mother taking the front seat, and his dad settled in the rear.

Austin asked, "How was the drive? Did you get my texts?"

"I didn't see the texts until after we arrived," his mom said. "You know that texting and driving isn't safe."

"But both of you weren't driving."

His parents were silent, and this only told Austin that they'd probably been discussing Everly.

"Look," Austin said. "Tonight is a big deal for me, and I was worried that something had happened on the drive. I knew that Jessica would be sad to miss her party too."

His mother sniffed. "I've talked to some of my neighbors to find out when their grandkids will be visiting. I've already arranged a play date for Jessica for next weekend."

"That's great," Austin said, although he was feeling peeved. The point he'd tried to make last Sunday was having Jessica grow up in a family neighborhood where friends were a natural occurrence.

On the way home from the dinner tonight, after they met Everly, he planned to break the news to them about the house he was interested in. Maybe tomorrow they could all tour it as well.

But when he pulled behind the craft shop, his mom said, "Where are we going?"

"Everly lives in an apartment above the craft store."

His mom clicked her tongue. "Really, Austin. I thought you were smarter than dating a gold-digger. This town is quaint, but you're a college educated, successful—"

"Mom," Austin cut in. "Everly went to college, and she's an amazing artist." He didn't admit that her time in college was a year, and she hadn't graduated, but that didn't matter to him.

"Marnie," his dad said. "We should just meet her. I'm sure Austin wouldn't date a gold-digger."

Thanks, Dad, Austin silently said. He pulled to a stop in the nearest parking spot by the back door.

"Is it the sex, Austin?" his mother said, her tone faint as if the word was distasteful to speak. "I understand that you're probably in need of . . . something, but bringing a woman into Jessica's life is another matter."

Austin clenched his jaw. "Mom, I'm an adult, and it's none of your business. But for your information, we're not having sex, and I'll never base a relationship on that again."

His mom's eyes popped wide. "I don't need to know about all the women . . ."

"Marnie," his dad cut in.

"Look." Austin rubbed at his temples. "You need to know something. Both of you. This is probably not the best timing to have this conversation, but since I'm now dating again, maybe it is the best timing."

Both of his parents stared at him.

"Rachel and I . . . Well, things weren't going so well," he said. "I had reservations when we were getting married, but my loyalty kept me committed. *She* didn't have such loyalty."

Still no response from his parents. The night was a velvety black, and the only light coming into the cab of the truck was the moonlight.

"Remember her friend Taylor she talked about? The one she stayed with once in a while?"

His mom nodded, and his dad said, "I remember."

"Taylor is a man, and they were lovers," Austin said bluntly. "I assumed she was a woman until I got a phone call a month after the funeral from Taylor himself. He wanted her stuff out of his apartment but didn't want to throw it away. I felt sick with suspicion, and Taylor confessed."

"Oh, Austin," his mother said, covering her mouth with her hand.

"It wasn't just an affair, though," Austin continued. "She was planning on divorcing me when Jessica was in first grade. Which would have only been about six months later. But then she got cancer."

Austin's voice had thickened, and although it had been nearly two years since that conversation with his wife's lover, he could feel the edges of the dark pain it had brought him.

His mother sniffled, and his dad reached across the seat for her hand.

"So for you, or anyone, to imply that my relationship with Everly is based on something it's not, is dead wrong. And I'll never put Jessica in a situation that would have her heart broken like I've had mine. Rachel's betrayal was worse than her death."

Neither of his parents spoke for a moment, and Austin was pretty sure he'd shocked them.

"I'm sorry about Rachel," his mother said, her face flushed. "We had no idea, and . . . of course you can date and not be drilled with questions."

He nodded. "Thank you."

"We'd love to meet Everly, son." His father placed a comforting hand on his shoulder.

His dad might be a man of few words, but when he did speak, everyone paid attention.

"I'll be back in a minute," he said, although he could have

just called Everly to come down. He felt like he had to give her some sort of head's up. Climbing out of the truck, he inhaled the cooling summer air. It felt good to be out of the small space with his parents, as terrible as that sounded.

The back door was unlocked because the craft store was still open. He went through, then hesitated at the *Do Not Enter* door that led to Everly's place. He texted her, then opened the door.

She appeared at the top of the stairs, fiddling with an earring.

"Hi," he said. "Sorry for barging in."

Her smile was easy. "It's okay, I'm ready. I just need to grab my purse."

"Purse? You mean . . . oh." She did have a small purse.

"Didn't want to scare your parents off with my giant bag," she said, coming down the stairs toward him.

Her dress was red with white paisley print, and it swished just above her knees. When she reached him, he smiled, the hard conversation with his parents starting to ebb.

"Hi," he said again.

Her hazel eyes studied him. "You already said hi. Is everything okay, Austin?"

"It is now," he said, and he meant it. Lifting his hand, he ran his fingers along her jaw, then lightly down her neck. "You look beautiful."

Everly still watched him, her brow furrowed. He pressed a kiss to her temple, then drew back and grasped her hand.

"Have you changed your mind about me meeting your parents?" she asked.

"Not at all," he said. "But I wanted to give you a head's up about my mom. On the drive over here, I told them about Rachel—the truth. All of it. So, they might be a bit, um, subdued."

Everly's eyes widened. "Goodness. That must have been a shock. And you thought you should tell them moments before meeting me?"

Austin's face warmed. "Yes. It was because my mom has been acting so possessive about Jessica, and so . . . I don't know how to say this . . ."

"She sees me as a threat because I live here, and you don't," Everly finished. "And if things keep progressing, then maybe you'll be so charmed by this small town, as well as a certain woman who lives in it, and decide to move here. And your mom will lose daily contact with her granddaughter."

He was pretty much speechless. "Wow. How did you guess?"

Everly lifted a shoulder. "I'm a woman, and I also have a mom who's a worrywart." She squeezed his hand. "Come on, I don't want to keep them waiting."

Austin nodded. "Right." As they headed into the back portion of the shop, he said, "Have I scared you off?"

Everly stopped and turned, lifting her chin to meet his gaze with a soft smile. "You're going to have to try harder than that, Mr. Architect."

Austin chuckled, then despite not wanting to mess up her lip gloss, he kissed her anyway. The kiss was over too soon, and Everly wiped the sheen of lip gloss from his mouth.

"Better?" he said.

"Yes, better." She nudged him. "Your parents are going to think we're up to no good. Better keep walking."

"We can't have them thinking that," he said with a wink.

Which meant that Everly's cheeks were flushed when they stepped out into the summer night. She was also still holding his hand, which he liked, very much. He led her to the back door so she could sit on the rear bench with his dad.

After opening the door, he made the introductions, and

Everly climbed into the truck, then shook each of his parent's hands.

By the time they reached the restaurant, Everly had told his parents about her family and her job. His mom had been mostly quiet, but his dad had asked questions, so Austin was at least grateful for that.

"Well, this is it," Everly said as they pulled up to a restaurant. "Chez Villiers is our fanciest restaurant in town. You'll love the owner. He's a crack up. His real name is Luis Waters, but since opening his restaurant, he insists on being called Louis Villiers."

"Is he French?" his dad asked.

Everly laughed. "No, but he sort of adopted himself into the culture. He's an excellent chef, although now he's hired other chefs since he's busy with running the place. Tonight will be busy with the Fourth of July tourists, so I made a reservation."

"Sounds nice," his mom said, although Austin couldn't read her tone.

They headed into the restaurant and were soon seated at a table for four. The flameless candles on the tables were a nice touch, and the soft Italian music playing added to the ambiance.

"Everly, darling," a dark-haired man said, striding toward them. He wore a double-breasted suit, and he was nearly as round as he was tall.

Everly rose to her feet and embraced the man. Then she turned and introduced everyone to Louis Villiers.

Everly was right. He did speak with a French accent, although Austin was pretty sure it was manufactured. He refrained from laughing at the guy and decided that his colorful personality matched the restaurant.

Otherwise, the food was excellent, and even his mom was complimentary.

"Austin says you run the local craft fair in your city," Everly said to his mom. "That must be a tremendous undertaking."

His mom was hesitant at first, but with Everly's continued questions, his mom started to open up.

"You should come to our fall festival," Everly said. "We have vendors from all over the state."

This piqued his mother's interest as she asked about the various vendors who attended. "My mother is on the committee, so I'm sure you'll have a lot to discuss when you meet."

His mom's brows arched at that.

"In fact, she asked me to invite you to her Sunday brunch," Everly continued. "We meet almost every week for a meal. Sometimes my other relatives will come, too."

"Perhaps," his mom said, at the same time his dad said, "We'd love to come."

His mom shot a glance at his dad, but this time his dad didn't go into his quiet mode. "Jessica has talked about your mom . . . What's her name again?"

"Lydia," Everly said.

"Ah," his dad said. "She kept saying Iddy, so I was curious."

"That's a new one," Everly said with a smile.

"So, Everly," his mom said as the waiter filled their water glasses, then cleared their main dishes. "You work at a craft store, and you're also an artist?"

"I'm a former artist," Everly said. "I was tired of painting and not selling anything." She shrugged and glanced at Austin with a sheepish smile.

He grasped her hand which was resting on the table.

"Austin thinks I should take it up again, but I don't know." She paused. "I mean, I don't want to be the proverbial starving artist."

"And you work at a craft store instead?"

Everly laughed good-naturedly. "Right? I know it sounds like I'm whiling away my days not doing much, but I love working retail. I guess I'm an odd duck. My mother has a beautiful home, but we get along better if we live separately."

His mom smiled, and it was genuine. "Of course. We've offered Austin a place with us multiple times. I know that Jessica would love it."

This was an old, worn-out argument between him and his parents, but he'd had to put his foot down somewhere.

"Jessica is a sweetheart," Everly said. "She's the type of kid who will always bloom where she's planted."

And it was the first time all night that Austin saw his mom relax.

"She is a dear," his mom agreed. "We're very lucky."

Everly smiled, and Austin squeezed her hand.

"So, what are your plans tomorrow?" Everly said. "I told Austin that you should come to the town breakfast at the park. There's a hometown parade, followed by a carnival. And of course, fireworks when it gets dark."

His mother nodded. "I'm sure Jessica will want to do all of it."

Everly laughed. "I've no doubt."

By the end of the evening, and by the time Austin was driving his parents back to their hotel after taking Everly home, he knew that his parents had warmed toward her.

Brad had texted him, asking if Jessica could stay one more hour since they'd all started watching *Ella Enchanted.*

So, this was Austin's chance to have a heart to heart with his parents. He had to complete this step before talking to Everly. He didn't want to make his parents feel like he'd alienated them.

"Hey, Mom and Dad," he said as he pulled into the hotel parking lot, "Can we talk for a moment?"

His mom nodded, and his dad said, "Sure thing."

"First of all," Austin said, "Thanks for coming to dinner with Everly and me. She definitely enjoyed meeting you."

"We enjoyed meeting her," his dad said. "I think she's a good person, and I can see that you care about her."

"I do," Austin said in a quiet voice. His mom hadn't said anything, so he looked over at her. "Mom?"

She sniffled, and he realized she was crying.

His stomach plummeted. "What's wrong?"

"Everly's, uh . . ." His mom fished out a tissue from her purse and dabbed at her cheeks. "She's . . . good for you, Austin. I can see it when you're together. Your countenance is lighter, and you're . . . happy. And I'm so sorry about misjudging and not knowing about Rachel. I can't imagine your pain."

Austin swallowed against the growing lump in his throat. "Mom," he said, grasping her hand. "Rachel is firmly in the past. She gave us Jessica, and I'll always be grateful for that."

His mom sniffled then nodded.

"Everly might not have a fancy degree or own a condo or house, but she's a genuine person," he said. "I'm happy with her, and I've felt things that I never thought I would."

His mom squeezed his hand, then released him and used her tissue to blow her nose.

His dad rested a hand his shoulder. "I think you'll do fine with her. And heaven knows, Jessica won't stop talking about her."

Austin chuckled, but his mom's emotions still had him on edge.

She wadded up the tissue and put it back into her purse. "We've been hoping you'd find a woman to help you raise Jessica," she said in a quiet tone. "But I never expected it to happen so soon, or to have such mixed feelings. I know that's something I need to work through."

Austin exhaled. "Mom, we've only been dating for a few

weeks, so it's a leap to say that she'll be helping me raise Jessica."

She reached over and patted his arm. "A mother knows these things, son."

He could only stare at her.

"Of course, it will be your decision," his mom continued, "and Everly's. But the writing is on the wall."

He glanced at his father, who only nodded.

Twenty-one

"I CAN'T WAIT ANY LONGER," Austin whispered in Everly's ear as they sat behind his parents at the firework show.

The town park was filled with spectators. Older people sat back in lawn chairs, young families spread out on blankets, teens huddled in groups, and toddlers stared at the sky in fascination as colors exploded across it.

"For what?" Everly whispered back, goosebumps racing across her skin at his nearness. They sat on a blanket by themselves since Jessica was curled on her grandpa's lap where they sat in lawn chairs that Everly had brought along. With Austin's parents' gazes glued to the fireworks, he'd been stealing kisses. And some of them had carried a bit of heat.

"To show you my surprise."

Everly smiled. "You've been dangling that in front of me all day. I'm sort of over it now."

Austin tugged her against him with a growl. "That's cruel."

She turned more fully in his arms, looping her arms about his neck. "You're cruel for tormenting me with whatever this surprise is."

"Let's go then," he said, resting his forehead against hers.

"What about your family?"

"Jessica wants to stay in the hotel tonight," he said. "I'll tell my mom we're leaving, then we'll head out."

Everly folded up the blanket while Austin talked to his mom. She turned and gave Everly a little wave, and she waved back. Then Austin was at her side again, taking the blanket, then grasping her hand. They wove their way through the onlookers. It had been a full day, a great day, starting with the early morning pancake breakfast. At the parade, Mr. Hayes had reunited with his cousins, and a lot of stories from long ago were swapped. Jessica hadn't seen Brock anywhere, and Brandy had texted both her and her mom that she was spending time at a bungalow on the beach about seven hours away.

Austin's mom had been right. Jessica had wanted to do everything, and frankly Everly was surprised the little girl was still awake.

A few people waved at Everly, their knowing glances flitting to Austin, but she didn't mind. She was in love with her fling, and there was no hiding that now. Probably the only one who didn't know was Austin himself. The thought sent a nervous laugh through her.

"What's funny?" Austin asked.

"Oh . . . nothing."

He didn't press her, and that was probably a good thing. They reached the truck, and Austin opened the passenger door for her, then set the blanket on the back seat. When he climbed into the driver's side, she asked, "Where are we going?"

His gaze cut to hers, and he smiled.

"You're not telling me?"

"Nope."

She gave a mock sigh. "You're like an excited little kid."

"Pretty much," he said with a chuckle.

There were no other cars on the road since the fireworks were still in full swing, and it soon became obvious that they were headed toward the theater. So, maybe it had something to do with the renovation.

Sure enough, Austin parked in front of the theater, then looked over at her.

"Ready?"

"We're watching a movie by ourselves?"

He grinned. "Good guess, but no." Then he opened his door and came around the truck to open hers.

She slid off the seat, and he grasped her hand. For some reason her heart was thumping hard as he led her to the dark building. Most of the town's businesses were closed down for the Fourth, and the movie theater was no exception, something that wouldn't have happened in a larger city.

He unlocked the side door, and they stepped into the darkness. Soon enough, he turned on lights, and the movie theater began to take shape. The first theater was completely done, and now that's where moviegoers were watching movies, and the second theater was nearly completed. Everly had seen the first theater's renovation, and she had to admit that she'd loved it.

The concessions were also updated, and the main lobby would go under construction next.

"Come on," Austin said, moving the taped barriers to the unfinished theater.

"Do I need a hardhat?" she teased.

"No, you'll be fine." There was a smile in his voice, but he sounded a tad nervous as well.

Then he tugged down a tarp that was covering the top of the inner doors leading into the theater room. Above the door was a wide brass name plate with the words inscribed: *The Bruce Kane Theater.*

Her dad.

"Austin!" she gasped. "What is this?"

"I talked to the mayor, and she agreed that we could dedicate the theater to your dad since he was such an avid patron."

Everly stared at the name plate as her eyes burned with tears. "I don't even know what to say, I can't believe it. My mom is going to be stunned."

"When we do the ribbon cutting for the grand re-opening, the mayor wants you and your family to say a few words about your dad."

Everly wiped at the tears that had fallen onto her cheeks, then she buried her head against Austin's chest and wrapped her arms about him. She was crying, but she didn't care. Austin pulled her tightly against him and pressed a kiss against her hair.

"I can't believe you did this."

He ran his hand slowly over her back, and after a few moments, he said, "I have another surprise for you, although this one you might not be thanking me for."

She drew away and looked at him, but he was smiling. "What is it?" she whispered, hardly daring to believe anything could stun her so much as the theater being named after her dad.

He linked their hands and led her through the theater doors. Inside, he turned up the lights all the way. The hallway leading to the theater screen and seats was newly painted a dark gray, and hanging on the wall was a series of framed pictures.

Everly stared at the posters from the craft store, posters of her paintings.

"Is this your choice of decoration?" she whispered, hardly able to talk.

"They're a placeholder for what I hope can be the real deal." Austin released her hand and pulled out a folded piece of paper from his back pocket. Then he unfolded the paper and handed it over.

Everly tore her gaze from the row of black and white pictures of iconic movie stars painted in black and white and looked down at the paper in her hand. It was an invoice signed by Mayor Sanders, and an attached check was at the bottom. For thousands of dollars.

"The town wants to commission my art for the theater?"

"Yeah," Austin said. "I showed the mayor your work, and she agreed that it would be perfect for the new theme of the theater. When I talked to her about the value of having original artwork, and not printed posters, she agreed to take my proposal to the budget committee."

Everly's hands were trembling, and her throat was too tight to respond.

"Yesterday, they approved it, and cut the check," Austin said. "The only question now is if you'll accept the commission."

She blinked back tears before they could drip onto the invoice she held. "Austin . . . this is . . . I . . ." She threw his arms about his neck and held on tight. "Yes, I'll do it. Yes!"

Austin chuckled as he scooped her close and lifted her off the ground. "Good. I'm so glad because I would have felt like an idiot in love if you'd said no."

Everly stilled. Had he just said . . . "Austin . . ."

"I love you, Everly," he rasped against her ear. "I know it's fast, and I know I've caught you off-guard, but it's the truth."

His words created a path of fire to her heart, and she was

pretty sure she was going to spontaneously ignite. Or cry. Or both. She drew away enough so that she could kiss him. He kissed her back, and soon he had her back up against the wall below her framed pictures. She gripped his shirt, holding him close, never wanting to release him. Each day with Austin only got better.

When they both had to breathe, Austin said, "I have one more surprise for you, babe, but it has to wait until tomorrow."

"You're killing me, Austin," she whispered as she moved her hand through his hair.

He grinned then pressed a soft kiss just beneath her jaw, his whiskers tickling her neck.

They spent another hour in the theater while Austin showed her the details of the renovations. And they might have kissed by the concessions and the ticket booth, and again in the finished theater while sitting in the middle seats of the middle row.

And it was a miracle that Everly slept at all, especially considering that Austin said he had another surprise for her. But when she woke up Sunday morning, she was also surprised to see that she'd slept until nine.

She scrambled out of bed and started the shower. She'd be meeting Austin and his family at her mom's place at ten for the brunch, and Everly had a feeling that her mom had invited more people than usual. Many in Town were curious about Austin as well as any updates on Brandy and Brock.

After her shower, Everly dressed carefully, choosing a summery dress in pale yellow. She checked her cell phone and saw that Austin had texted a couple of times. Everly grinned as she read them.

Good morning, gorgeous.
Still sleeping?

Do you want me to pick you up?

She wrote back. *I slept in. I'll meet you there.* Then she added a heart emoji. It wasn't lost on her that Austin had told her he loved her, but she hadn't said it back. She knew she was in love with him, but she also wanted to tell him separately and not in response to him telling her.

She hoped he wasn't annoyed about that, but his plentiful kissing last night and his texts this morning told her he wasn't. Everly wasn't even sure her feet touched the ground as she hurried down the stairs after feeding Snatches.

Not only was she looking forward to the brunch, and being with Austin and his family, but starting tomorrow, she was going to order the art supplies to get started on the paintings. She was a genuine commissioned artist now. A working artist! It was still mind-boggling, and she doubted she'd ever get used to the fact. Laughing at herself, she pulled onto Main Street and headed toward her mom's.

Apparently, she was the last to arrive, and she walked past the Hayes' tan minivan and Austin's white truck on the way.

She didn't knock or ring the doorbell, instead she walked into her mom's home. Sure enough, Aunt Janice and Uncle Stanley were there, along with several of her cousins. Also, a few Hayes were there, not ones in Brock's direct family, thank goodness.

"Everly!" Jessica called out, and ran to her.

Everly hugged the little girl. "How was the hotel?"

"I got to sleep on a rolled bed," Jessica stated proudly. "And Grandma did my braids." She turned around to show her two French braids.

"Very pretty," Everly said. "I love them." She caught Mrs. Hayes watching them from across the room.

Mrs. Hayes smiled, and Everly smiled back.

Then Austin showed up at her side. He slipped an arm about her waist and kissed her cheek. "Hello, beautiful."

Everly's cheeks warmed. "Hi, handsome."

He chuckled and tightened his hold around her waist. "Your mom has been talking my mom's ear off. I can't decide who's the bigger committee queen."

Everly looked over to where her mom was in conversation with the larger group that included the Hayes cousins. The food was great, and the conversation lively. Everly's favorite part was how Austin stayed close to her, either holding her hand, or keeping his arm about her chair.

She knew that her mom was taking surreptitious glances at them, but Everly didn't mind.

As the brunch wound down and most people were heading out the door, Austin said, "I want you to take a walk with me."

"Okay," Everly said, meeting his gaze. The request wasn't totally strange, but the timing was. "Just me?"

"All of us, in fact," he said. Then he also invited his parents and her mom.

So, the whole crew set off down the sidewalk, Jessica skipping along. Austin told everyone they'd just have to wait and see where they were going. They walked through the quiet streets, beneath the rows of trees lining the sidewalks. About two streets down, Austin turned into another neighborhood.

"Hey, this is where Lizzy lives," Jessica said. "Are we going to Lizzy's?"

"Not today," Austin said, squeezing Everly's hand.

Their mothers were talking about the upcoming fall festival, and Mr. Hayes had grabbed Jessica's hand.

Then Everly saw it—a house two doors down that had a For Sale sign on the front lawn. It was one of those older homes that looked like it had gone through some extensive renovations already. Not that Austin couldn't handle renovations . . . What was he thinking? As they neared the house, her heart was trying to gallop out of her chest.

Because her initial thoughts couldn't be true, could they?

When Austin turned up the walk to the house, tears burned in her eyes, and she couldn't have spoken if someone offered another art commission.

He stopped on the porch, released her hand, then produced a key to unlock the front door. No one said anything as he pushed the door open and stepped inside.

"Well, come in and tell me what you think," he said, motioning for them to come inside.

"This is the old Anderson home," her mom murmured, stepping past Everly. "It's been changed a lot, though."

Everly stepped into the entry, but still couldn't speak as everyone filed past her, walking into the kitchen, the living room. Mr. Hayes wandered down the hall with Jessica asking a million questions a minute as she held onto her grandpa's hand. His murmured voice faded, and the women were opening the pantry doors in the kitchen, then they went out the kitchen door that led to the back yard.

Austin shut the front door and gazed over at her.

She couldn't meet his gaze though. Her heart had moved into her throat, and she looked about the rooms with blurry vision. What was Austin doing? Why had he brought them all here to look at this house? The answer was like a fiery dart to her mind, but she couldn't grasp it all.

Finally, she turned to see him leaning against the front door, watching her, those brown eyes of his intent on her every movement, every reaction.

"What did you do, Austin?" she whispered.

"I put in an offer this morning," he said. "And the realtor let me have the key for the day to show everyone around.

Assuming my offer is accepted, I'll be relocating Jessica and I here at the end of the month."

Everly opened her mouth, then closed it. "Why?"

"I think I told you why last night." He straightened from the door and walked toward her.

She was rooted to the floor. Couldn't move. Wouldn't move.

When Austin stopped in front of her, he cradled her face with his hands. "I love you, Everly, and I want to be where you are." The edges of his mouth curved in the way she loved so much. "And I want my daughter to have a real home in a great neighborhood. So, I'm hoping you like this house too, because I have plans for us. If, that is, it's okay with you."

He leaned down and pressed the softest kiss on her mouth. "What do you say, Everly Kane?"

She curled her fingers in his shirt. "I like the house, Austin."

"Good," he murmured, kissing her again.

"And I love you," she whispered. "So much."

He smiled then. "I was hoping you felt that way. Or else things might be a bit awkward when we're both trying to stake out the middle seats at the theater."

She laughed, and it might have been a little bit of crying too. But Austin had started kissing her again, and she ran her hands up his chest, then locked her arms about his neck.

"Grandpa, look!" Jessica called out. "They're kissing!"

A deep chuckle sounded from Mr. Hayes, but Austin didn't release her.

"Let's go see Grandma in the backyard," Mr. Hayes said. "I think I spied a swing set."

"Really?" Jessica squealed.

Running footsteps, followed by the quiet click of a closing door, then silence.

They were alone again, and Austin had drawn away, his gaze holding her captive as his thumb traced the edge of her jaw.

"I don't think I can take any more surprises, Austin," Everly whispered as warmth buzzed along her skin, pooling in her belly.

Austin's eyes darkened as his mouth lifted into a half smile. "I think you need to get used to them," he rumbled. "Because I've fallen in love with my fling."

Everly laughed, then let him draw her back into his arms, his touch, his scent, his world, and she decided that she'd always welcome surprises from Austin.

Heather B. Moore is a four-time *USA Today* bestselling author. She writes biblical fiction under the pen name H.B. Moore, such as *Esther the Queen* and *Ruth*. Under the name Heather B. Moore, she writes romance and women's fiction. Her newest releases include the historical novels *The Paper Daughters of Chinatown* and *The Slow March of Light*. She's also one of the coauthors of the *USA Today* bestselling series: A Timeless Romance Anthology. Heather writes speculative fiction under the pen name Jane Redd; releases include the Solstice series and *Mistress Grim*. Heather is represented by Dystel, Goderich & Bourret.

For book updates, sign up for Heather's email list: hbmoore.com/contact

Website: HBMoore.com
Facebook: Fans of Heather B. Moore
Blog: MyWritersLair.blogspot.com
Instagram: @authorhbmoore
Pinterest: HeatherBMoore
Twitter: @HeatherBMoore

Made in United States
Orlando, FL
07 September 2023